BOBBINS AND BODIES

ACF BOOKENS

1

I had been watching the old house tip over for about three months now. It was one of the eighteenth-century farmhouses in our region of Virginia, a carryover from the Germans who made their way to Octonia County from Pennsylvania and stopped here before settling in more numbers over in the Shenandoah Valley.

The building was a thing of beauty – a stone foundation, graying old timbers, solid, hand-hewn doors, and a porch that opened with a view to the Blue Ridge. But like many other big houses in the area, it was just too much upkeep for too little return. A couple houses of similar size nearby had been completely remodeled and one had become an Airbnb but, by and large, the families around here wanted more space or less draftiness. So houses like this one, they were becoming scarce as they caved in on themselves.

When I heard through the historians' grapevine of social media and police scanners that the house was going to be taken down, I looked up the owners and asked if I could come salvage what I could. I offered them the highest price I was able, but they quickly refused money and said they'd just be happy to see parts of the house used elsewhere. Turns out, they were only taking it down because they were afraid it might fall down on their grandkids and really wished they had the funds to restore it. I knew, as did they, that such an undertaking was one of love, not of financial return and, as is the case for most of us, love didn't buy their groceries.

I knew next to nothing beyond what I learned on *Barnwood Builders* and *Salvage Dawgs* about how to take down a house, so, really, I knew nothing. But fortunately, my dad knew something about old buildings and, even more fortunately, his friend Saul knew everything about taking them down. Saul was one of my favorite people, and my best friend, Mika's, uncle, so he was the first person I called when I got permission to salvage.

"Beef up your insurance, Paisley-girl," Saul said as soon as I told him what I wanted to do. "High as it will go. You can't be leaving that boy without his mama."

"That boy" was my almost-three-year-old son Sawyer, and Saul was right. I was doing this work because it kept my schedule flexible to be with Sawyer as much as possible while also providing us much-needed income when I sold the salvaged wares. Thus far, I hadn't gotten behind on any payments, and my list of newsletter subscribers was growing, which meant that I might soon be able to leverage some of this work into other work.

But a higher insurance package wasn't part of my budget, and I guess Saul heard the quaking silence after his suggestion because he said, "Okay, then, you'll lead one of my crews. Welcome to the team. Come down to the yard and sign the paperwork as soon as you get the chance." I heard the phone drop into the cradle – Saul didn't believe in cell phones – and sat there on the dead line for a minute.

"What is it?" Mika asked. I had made the call from the wingback chairs at the front of her yarn store since I was there to fulfill our agreement for Saturdays, the day Sawyer was with his dad. I helped with customers and straightened up the store, and she held me accountable to get some work done instead of just surfing the internet and buying a million (more) cross-stitch patterns.

"Saul just hired me," I murmured.

"I'm sorry. Did you just say my Uncle Saul just hired you?" She sat down hard in the chair across from me, her black hair bouncing forcefully against her shoulders. Mika was one of those people who looked great in the latest fashion trends, which meant she looked like she wasn't even aware she was being trendy. With her peachy porcelain skin and a spattering of freckles across her nose, she was gorgeous without pretense or effort. She was beautiful, and while she knew it, she didn't really care. "Tell me I misheard you," she said.

I pulled my rolled bandana down over my face and then slid it back up to tuck my wayward strands into place again. Unlike my best friend, I had never mastered the latest styles or trends in fashion or in hair. I tended to just wear it down or throw it up if it got in my eyes. Combine my casual hair with the slight gray pallor to my complexion that was brought on by late nights of work and full days of parenting a robust toddler, and I felt anything but robust myself. Still, I did feel beautiful because, for the first time in my life, I was doing just what I wanted to do with my life instead of building my life around someone else's . . . well, except the someone else who stood just over three feet tall and made my day with his laugh. But I was okay with that – more than okay, in fact. Gleeful, even at forty-six when parenting a toddler was just about at the edge of my physical limits, it was still the most amazing thing I'd ever done.

"Your uncle just hired me. You heard me correctly, but I can barely believe it myself," I replied.

Mika's Uncle Saul hung the moon as far as Mika and I were concerned, but he was a gruff guy. Mika had once told me that he didn't believe in barbers and cut his own wiry silver hair with his pocketknife. From the look of the gray stubble against his leathery skin, I wondered if he also shaved with that knife. And the people – mostly men – who worked for him were, let's just say, not exactly primed and ready for a day at the country club. The idea of me working with that group, well, it was pretty laughable. Beyond the fact that I loved good overalls and comfy flannels, those guys and I had little in common.

"Yep. He wants me to come and work for him so that I'll be covered by his insurance while we do that house job I told you about." I picked up my glass of white wine and sighed. "If I was smart, I'd take him up on it."

Mika stared at me for a minute and then sighed. "That man will do anything for anyone, but for you, he's offering space on his crew. That's really something." Saul had given Mika the seed money for her business, told her it was a no-interest loan with no due date, and every time she paid him back a little of the sum he loaned her, he sent one of the women from his office into the store and bought exactly the amount she'd given him back in stock, which he then gave to a group of local knitters who made slippers for women and children in shelters through the Pink Slipper Project. And of course, he donated the yarn in Mika's name.

Thus, each time she paid him, he paid her back and then doubled the gift. It was something Mika didn't talk about much because she really did wish he'd just accept her payments, as a matter of pride, but mostly because she knew Saul wouldn't like people knowing about it. He was one of those people who really followed that Bible lesson about not letting your left hand know what your right hand was doing when it came to good works.

I stretched out my legs and put my feet on the small ottoman between the two chairs and said, "Actually, he offered me the chance to *lead* one of his crews."

Mika sat up. "You're kidding!? Man, that guy just doesn't know when to quit." She was smiling, but I knew she was also worried. I could see the concern in the way the furrow between her eyebrows deepened just a little. We'd been friends since college, since before either of us had that permanent wrinkle in our foreheads, and I knew my best friend. She was worried.

"You don't think I can lead his crew?" I asked with every desire to keep defensiveness out of my voice. I thought I did pretty good.

But then Mika laughed. "And clearly you don't either." She reached over and began to massage my foot. "You are so good at so many things, Paisley Sutton, but leading? Not so much. You're more of a lone wolf kind of worker."

I probably wouldn't have objected to her comment anyway because she was right, but she was working out a week's worth of my single parenting and money stress with her thumbs. I didn't want to cross her and risk jeopardizing my massage, so I stayed quiet.

"I, however, know most of those guys from poker nights with my dad." She stopped rubbing my feet and took out her phone. "When's your salvage job?" she asked without looking up.

"I have no idea, Miks. I just found out your uncle is giving me a crew."

"Great. Tuesday and Wednesday it is. I'll ask Mrs. Stephenson if she can watch the store. She's been looking for some part-time hours, and I could use the help anyway. This is a great chance for me to trust someone else with the store." She shivered a little as she said it.

I had about a million objections, including the fact that I would have to ask my dad and his wife Lucinda to watch Sawyer for two full days in a row. But Mika was kind of bouncing in her chair as she looked at me, and the fact that she was willing to let a good-souled but extremely bossy knitter like

Ms. Stephenson staff the store told me she was more than eager. I didn't want to disappoint her, and Saul had offered me a crew. Plus, I really needed the potential infusion of cash that the sale of the wood would mean.

"Okay, Tuesday and Wednesday it is. Now, I just need to learn how to tear down a house."

FORTUNATELY, Mika was, unlike me, a great leader, and the next day she took it on herself to get together with her Uncle Saul over dinner and some apple pie moonshine. By the time they were both pretty lit, they had a safe and solid plan for taking down the old house. And Monday morning, after Mika sobered up, the sketches for the process arrived in my inbox.

Sawyer, who had been entirely engrossed in cooking me a three-course meal that included kiwi, snake, and ice cream from his toy kitchen, immediately sensed that I was focusing on something and climbed into my lap at my computer. "What that, Mama?" he asked in his "still toddler but getting less so" voice.

"It's pictures of a house Auntie Mika and I are going to take down," I said. It's always a question for me – how to tell the truth without over-telling.

Sawyer jumped up, ran across the living room, and then climbed back into my lap . . . with his toolbox. "I ready."

I squeezed my sweet boy close and said, "Yes, you are, Love Bug. Why don't we practice with some blocks?"

He furrowed his brow and looked at me. "Okay. But then we do house." He wasn't asking.

I climbed down to the floor, which seemed to be getting further and further away the deeper into my forties I got, and opened Sawyer's bag of blocks. "Love Bug, you can't come when we take the house down. It's dangerous."

He stared at me for a second and then said, "One minute. I

have idea," as he held one finger in front of my face before running up the stairs to his room. When he came back, he had on a little blue hard hat that I'd picked up at a yard sale. "Now, I ready."

I laughed. "Smart move, Little Man. Smart move." Rather than trying to dissuade him from his plan and also trying to explain the concept of tomorrow to a child who did not yet understand time, I let the house plans disappear as we built towers that were repeatedly demolished just as I was getting proud of them.

But once Sawyer was fast asleep in his bed for his nap, I opened my laptop and studied the plans. That's when I realized I was in *way* over my head. I didn't know the least thing about how to remove beams or even take out doorframes. The TV folks made it look simple, just a crowbar and a hammer, but clearly, there was much more involved. Thank goodness for Uncle Saul and thank goodness for cross-stitch and *Broadchurch* or I would have worried all night about what I'd gotten myself into.

Fortunately, I was starting a new cross-stitch project – a snow-covered barn pattern – something I'd picked up because it reminded me of my mom. I spent the evening getting my cloth ready and sorting the thread onto a piece of cardboard that would keep it from tangling and let me find the colors easily. Each time I picked up a hank of floss, my Maine Coon cat, Beauregard, swatted at it, and eventually I had to pry him up off my lap and onto his very own fleece blanket on the other end of the couch. The cat was entirely lazy unless he could be entirely annoying. But eventually, sloth won out, and he began his twentieth hour of sleep for the day while I stitched myself to calm.

. . .

The next morning, Sawyer and I were up bright and early for bacon and pancakes from scratch, since Sawyer really wanted to cook. He poured the flour and dry ingredients, cracked the eggs, stirred in the milk and chocolate chips, and even told me when the butter was melted. But of course, he didn't eat a bite of his pancakes. Still, I figured grapes, chocolate milk, and four slices of bacon was an almost-balanced meal and loaded him into the car.

Before going to bed the night before, I'd sent my dad a text and then sent the same text, with a preamble, to my stepmom to be sure my dad got it. Lucinda got right back to me and said, *Your dad says that sounds like a great plan. See you at seven forty-five.*

So now we were on our way to my dad and Lucinda's house so that they could supervise Sawyer, on-site, while his mama tried her best not to get killed taking down a house. Sawyer loved "big equipment," and Saul's plan involved a crane, a bucket truck, and a skid steer, so I knew my son would be in hog heaven. My dad, too. Lucinda was just coming along for moral support and to be sure my dad didn't let Sawyer do anything too dangerous, like drive the crane. My dad was great with his grandson, but his threshold for danger was far higher than mine. Thank goodness Lucinda and I agreed that using a nail gun wasn't really fitting until Sawyer was in college.

Dad and Lucinda were on their porch when we arrived, and, as usual, they climbed into the back seat to play with their grandson, while his royal highness, Beauregard, claimed the towel (and the seat warmer) in the front seat. Dad had long ago given up trying to win the battle against the cat – and besides, this way, he could tickle Sawyer for the whole drive.

Lucinda had this great quirky sense of style that often meant pairing sweatpants with a nice sweater, a chunky piece of jewelry, and gorgeous, dangling earrings purchased from a fair-trade market. It was kind of like she was always dressed for a Zoom meeting but never had any. The fact that she had married my dad was stunning because my dad was still wearing clothes that he'd worn when I was in high school over thirty years earlier. But the two of them were deeply in love, and it made me happy to see them together. As I drove and Beauregard slept, I watched them revel in Sawyer's enthusiastic story about how he was going to climb up to the top of the house and jump down with Baby, his doll. As soon as he could sit still for more than five minutes, I was going to have that boy watch *Spider-Man.*

When we pulled up to the house site, Saul and Mika were already there, and behind us on the dirt road, I could see a few pickup trucks on their way. We were out in force, and I knew the owners would appreciate the quick work we were, hopefully, going to make of it.

"Building's sound as can be, Paisley," Saul said as I climbed out of the car. "Give her a look and let us know what you definitely want and what will be good if we can get." I had made a list of ideas based on what I had seen in other farmhouses like this, but I had no idea what was actually there, much less salvageable.

I looked at Mika with what I knew must have been a look of panic, but she only smiled and said, "Let's get to it. Time's a-wasting."

I now realized the other reason I was glad Lucinda was along – for my moral support. Clearly, my best friend had begun channeling her wonderful, but abrasive, uncle, and I wasn't sure how I felt about that.

As uncle and niece glowered at me, I reached back into the car for my to-go mug of coffee. They might be in a hurry, but no one wanted me to make decisions of any kind without caffeine. Mika knew this, so when I stared back at her, she shrugged and even shot me a small smile as she followed behind me with a flowered clipboard in her hand and a pencil behind her ear.

I flung up a wave and blew Sawyer a kiss before marching toward the front door of the house.

"That one of Saul's?" I asked as we stopped just inside. I tapped my fingers on the bottom of her clipboard.

She rolled her eyes. "I thought I might as well take myself seriously in this job, you know."

"Okay, and also it was a chance to shop for 'school supplies.'" I reached over and took her pencil. "Yep, just as I figured. Sharpened to a fine point and only used on one side so your letters will take on the slanty look of calligraphy."

Mika snatched her pencil back but then looked at me. "How did you know?"

"Used to do the same thing myself," I said with a smile and looked around.

"This lintel here—" I pointed to the thick, wide beam spanning the house door. "That I definitely want. And same with these beams here." The house had never been Sheetrocked on the ceiling, so I could see the very wide beams holding up the second story. They were gorgeous.

As we walked, I pointed to all the major structural pieces of the house that I could easily see and told Mika that I wanted as many of them as we could safely take down. "And the siding, I'd like at least some of it. Dad has some ideas for some tables and things that he thinks we could sell locally."

I scuffed my feet against the hardwoods below and winced when a cloud of dust came up. These were shot, and as we walked into the second room, I could see that the floor had fallen down in most of the room. Still, there was a lot of good stuff in here, including a gorgeous mantel over the fireplace.

Mika scribbled every time I pointed something out, and when we stepped near a window, I could see she was marking each item I noted on a 3D rendering of the house. "That's impressive," I said.

"Uncle Saul had one of his guys take my sketch and put it in

CAD." She looked at me. "That's what the software is called, right?"

I shrugged. "You're asking me about a piece of software?"

"Good point," she said. "Thanks for letting me help, by the way."

I smiled. "Letting you? I'm pretty sure I would have been out of luck for workspace if I said no." I pushed my shoulder into Mika's. "So glad I'm smarter than that, and I'm really grateful to you and Saul. Didn't he have any other construction projects going on?"

Saul ran a really big construction company in Octonia. His crews built houses and churches, schools, and office buildings. His reputation was impeccable, and he was always in demand.

"Nah. The month of December is usually pretty quiet, he said. Nobody wants to start anything new before the end of the year, and he works hard to be able to give his guys December off, with pay, if they want to take a break." Mika made a note about the unpainted wainscotting and said, "Think your dad could do something with this?"

"Sure could," Saul said as he came up beside me. "You women almost ready? The crew's here, and daylight's wasting."

"Yep. Anything else, Pais?" Mika asked.

I was about to say we were good to go, when something caught my eye over in the opposite corner of the room down below floor level. Most of my salvage jobs were in houses and stores, places where people spent a lot of time. So I'd gotten good at looking in corners and under cabinets. The best stuff – jewelry, old photos, vintage toys – often ended up there.

Over in the corner beside the window, where the shadows got dark, I could just see the smallest arc of white. At first, I thought it might just be a sunbeam, but as I picked my way across the rotting floor, the more I could see it had shape and substance. It was small, like a crumpled piece of paper or a pen sticking out of the dirt.

I knelt down and bent low . . . and then I scrambled backwards on my hands and feet, kicking up a cloud of dirt and crumbling wood in my wake. "Oh no!" was all I could manage to say.

Mika reached down and dragged me to my feet. "What is it, Paisley?"

I pointed and then stared at my hand a minute. "It's a finger. A human finger." I took a long, deep breath and took a step forward again.

Saul put his hand on my shoulder and held me back as he stepped closer, leaned over, and said, "Time to call Sheriff Shiflett. No work today."

He took off his hat and stood staring at the finger while Mika dialed the sheriff's cell number. I thought I could hear Saul whispering a prayer.

2

My text to Dad and Lucinda was very simple: *Take Sawyer to a playground now. Police on their way. I don't want him to see this.*

Lucinda's text showed that she clearly heard the tone in my screen-locked words: *Headed to the goat house. We will keep him busy, get him his nap, and see you at the farmhouse later. Call if you need me.*

I let out a sigh and then slumped against the wall, glad that my little guy was going to his favorite playground with two of his favorite people. As I lifted my head to stare at the gorgeous tin ceiling above me and lament not only the loss of income but also the loss of life, a strong hand grasped my shoulder. "You okay?" Santiago Shifflett asked quietly.

I turned to face him and saw that he was in full sheriff's attire, gun and radio included. Just his presence, as sheriff and his kind self, was enough to slow my heart rate and help me take a deep breath. Shifflett was our county's first Latino sheriff, and while I knew he took some grief for that, I was very happy we had finally gotten over our racism, at least in this small way.

His affable but professional demeanor and quiet charm had won over a lot of people, me included. But today, I was just grateful for the concern in his deep brown eyes and the fact that he could wear a five o'clock shadow at eight a.m. and look good, not just scruffy.

I tried to put a smile on my face as I answered his question. "I am. Mostly." I pointed across the room. "But that person is definitely not okay."

Santiago squeezed my shoulder as he tilted his head toward Mika, who was staring very pointedly out the window. "Why don't you two go outside? I put some blankets on the hood of my car and left a thermos of hot cocoa there, too." He squeezed my shoulder and then strode toward the body.

I slipped my arm through Mika's and pretended I didn't see her wipe away tears as I led her out of the house and to the sheriff's car, where warmth waited.

We each took a wool blanket, and I grabbed the thermos. Then, we climbed up onto a round hay bale off in the field next to the house and cuddled up. Without even asking, I knew that Mika wouldn't want to leave. We were the same this way – responsible and curious to a fault.

As I poured her the first mug of cocoa, I said, "Remember when I lived up in Maryland for a while in that little townhouse neighborhood?"

Mika squinted and then nodded. "I do. Cute house. Strange neighbors."

"I know, right? Well, one day, two friends and I were cleaning up trash along the nature trail behind the neighborhood, and we found a bone, a long leg bone."

Mika sat up from where she'd been leaning on my shoulder. "You found a bone? Why am I just hearing about this now?"

I shrugged. "We freaked out, and I called the police. A deputy came over, took one look, and said, 'Dog.' Just like she'd seen this kind of thing a hundred times and felt confident enough in her canine forensic skills to be sure." I still remembered that deputy's placid face as she assured us multiple times that it wasn't a human femur.

"Oh my goodness. You trusted she was right? Didn't you want her to test it or something?" Mika asked.

"She was so sure that her confidence put us at ease. And when she sent the county maintenance staff to come clean up the remains, they found a collar." I was still grateful that the deputy had taken the time to call me when they did, just to reassure me.

"Someone just dumped their dog?" Mika's voice was squeaky.

"Actually, Sparky had dug his way out of my neighbor's yard because he wanted to chase a squirrel. But his collar got caught . . ." I didn't finish the sentence. It was a pet lover's worst nightmare.

"Poor Sparky. His owners must have been devasted."

I nodded and let out a long sigh. "They lived a couple doors down. You might remember them because they're the ones who drove the pink camo car."

Mika laughed. "How could I forget?"

"It took them a while," I said, "but eventually, they got a new pup, a Great Dane that they named Cletus. He was amazing with those floppy ears and long tail. The kids in the family had to walk him for hours a night just to get him enough exercise, but he loved those children."

"At least that story has a happy ending." Mika's eyes shifted from me to the front of the house, where a stretcher with a body bag was being rolled toward the coroner's van. "I don't think they'd use the stretcher for a dog, do you?"

As I watched them load the body in the van, I shook my head. "No. I had been hoping though."

"Me, too," Mika said as she put her head on my shoulder. "Thanks for the story. It was a good distraction."

I put my head on top of hers. "For me, too."

We both sat up as Santiago approached. "Not much I can tell you. I know you know that, but we will be launching an investigation which means . . ." He looked at me and gave me a sad smile.

"Which means this is a crime scene, so I can't salvage here until you've cleared the scene." I put my hands on top of my head and tried to keep my list of bills from scrolling through my mind like a news show's ticker tape.

"Oh no, Paisley!" Mika reached over and took my hands.

I squeezed her fingers. "It's okay. I'll make do. A murder investigation is definitely more important than my finances."

"I don't know about that," Santiago said. "The person who died is most important, of course, but the investigation doesn't need to outweigh everything. Also, who said anything about murder?"

Mika rolled her eyes. "Okay, Mr. Policeman . . . we'll just act like someone ends up buried in a house by accident."

Santiago cleared his throat, and I laughed. "She has a point," I said.

"She does. Yes, it was murder . . . but that is really all I can say." He looked me in the eyes. "You okay, really?"

I took a minute, checked in with myself, and found I was, indeed, okay. Sad. Shaken. But okay. "I am. Thank you for asking."

Santiago and I weren't dating, but we weren't not dating, not really. We'd spent a lot of time together a few weeks back because of a police matter that I'd inadvertently stumbled into. Since then, though, we'd had a couple of meetups over coffee and some fun text exchanges, but nothing more.

I was fine with that, mostly, because I wasn't sure I was ready to date. My divorce had been final for a couple of months, but I still was leery of getting into a new relationship, especially with Saw in the picture. That boy did love this policeman, though, and not just because of the flashing lights and siren. Santiago just seemed to get Sawyer, and I appreciated that a great deal.

"Do y'all need a ride home?" the sheriff asked.

"I have my car, so I'll take Paisley," Mika said. "But first, do you mind if we let Saul know what's going on?"

"You'll save me the trouble," Santiago said and gave me another squeeze on the arm before turning back to the house.

I took a deep breath and met Mika's gaze as we made our way over to her uncle and his crew. Mika jerked her head to the right, and Saul broke away from the cluster of men to join us a few feet away. "So it is a murder?"

Mika and I both nodded. "Yeah. The sheriff couldn't tell us more," Mika said, "but definitely a murder. We have to clear out so that they can process the scene."

I sighed and said, "I'm so sorry, Saul. I pulled you and your guys all the way out here—"

He interrupted me. "Did you murder that poor soul, Paisley?"

I took a step back. "No, of course not."

Saul stared at me intently. "Then why are you apologizing?" He kept staring at me until I shrugged.

"Sorry. Bad habit." I groaned. "See?"

"We actually have a clean-up job we can squeeze in now, so no harm, no foul, for us. And we're clear for the next two weeks, so whenever the site is ready, we'll just come on back." He glanced over his shoulder at the guys behind him, most of them with Styrofoam cups of coffee still steaming in their hands. "I do need to tell them something, though. Okay if I clue them in?"

Mika and I looked at each other and decided, silently, that Saul might as well let them know. It would be all over town by afternoon anyway, and maybe directness would slow the Octonia rumor train. I doubted it, but maybe.

The three of us walked over to the huddle of six men, and each of them nodded at Mika and me before turning to Saul. "Job's off for today, boys. It was a murder. Nothing more to know just now, but when I know and can tell you, I will. Now, let's head to the Jeffries site and get that job done while we have the space."

Most of the men nodded and began walking back to their vehicles, but one guy stayed around. I didn't recognize him, but he was about twenty years younger than me, so I probably wouldn't have known him unless he was a knitter who visited Mika's shop on Saturdays. From the look of his hands and the cracks in the callouses, I doubted yarn work was his deal. "Boss, guy who used to live up here went missing a few years back. Think I should tell the sheriff."

"What was the guy's name, Peter?" Saul asked.

"Rocket Sutherland, I mean Stephen Sutherland, Boss. We just called him Rocket."

Mika spoke up. "Do we want to know why you called him Rocket?"

I cringed because this conversation could get awkward really fast.

Peter blushed and said, "It was only because he could climb anything really quickly. He just rocketed up there."

I let out a breath I hadn't realized I was holding and smiled. "I do think the sheriff would like to hear about his disappearance. You said he was from up this way?"

"Yes, ma'am." Peter gestured up the gravel road that we'd all traveled in on. "Up a mile or so further into the mountains. Most folks thought he'd just left town, went to the city to get better work or something, but those of us who knew him had other ideas. Just didn't seem like Rocket to leave, especially to leave his girl."

Before I even knew I was going to ask I said, "Who was his girl?"

"Renee Morris. They'd been dating since high school. Rocket had bought her a ring and all. Just hadn't gotten the right time to ask, I guess," Peter said with a shrug.

I nodded. "Thanks, Peter. I'm sorry, I didn't catch your last name." He'd never said it, of course, because why would he? I wanted to know, though, just in case in mattered. Around here, manners were paramount, and I figured he'd answer my question out of politeness if nothing else.

"Peter Werzer, ma'am."

I put out my hand. "Nice to meet you. I'm Paisley Sutton."

"Yes, ma'am," he said as he gave me a firm handshake. "Known your father a long time. He and my granddad are good friends."

I smiled and tried not to wince. My dad was now friends with the grandfathers of people in their twenties. I was clearly much older than my mental age of twenty-seven.

"If you're done with the interrogation, Paisley, perhaps Peter here might go tell the actual police what he knows," Saul said with his eyebrows raised.

"Of course. Sorry," I said.

Saul gave me a hard stare at my giving yet another apology. "Call me when we're ready to get back to work," Saul said. Then he turned without waiting for a response and walked to his truck.

Mika bumped against me. "You ready to go?"

I stared at the house and then at the brick ranch house the owners lived in just beyond it. "Do you have a few minutes? I'd like to talk to the owners and see if I can learn a bit more about the house before we go."

"You mean, see if they know anything about the body buried there?" Mika said as she looked at me through narrowed eyes.

"Well, if that happens to come up . . ." I moved toward the house before she could say anything else.

But they weren't home. They'd left me a note on their front door with a number to call if we needed anything, but said they'd decided to be away for a few days since it was hard to see the house come down. A tiny part of me was suspicious about that, given the body that we'd found, but I didn't think people would bring in a crew to take down a house if they knew someone was buried there . . . and, also, I could relate to the sadness of losing a building you loved. It had happened to me more than once in my life.

"You're off the hook for a history lesson," I said to Mika as I walked back to meet her at her car. "They aren't home."

She snapped her fingers and said, "Darn. You know how I love to learn obscure dates and random facts about buildings."

"I do know." I smiled. Mika acted as if she didn't care, but she loved this place we called home as much as I did. While her thing was the people who lived here now, she'd been in Octonia long enough to appreciate that it wasn't just the *now* that made this place special. It was the *then*, too. She did bristle sometimes when people discounted her opinion because she'd only lived here a few years, but she was learning to understand that even that sort of snobbery was based on love of place.

She didn't have my unending love of research, though, so I was quite surprised when she said, "Feel like seeing if Rocket Sutherland's family is home?"

"Really? You want to go ask questions?"

She shrugged. "I'm paying Mrs. Stephenson for the whole day whether I'm there or not, so I might as well enjoy my time off."

"We could go get lunch, visit that new spa in town," I said with a smirk.

"Neither you nor I can afford a meal out, and while a massage sounds amazing, we need a windfall before either of us is getting a professional one of those." She laughed. "So let's go get this out of your system, and then we can swap shoulder rubs at your place before Sawyer gets home."

"That sounds perfect." I climbed into her passenger seat and said, "Onward!"

But I had no idea what exactly I was urging us toward, no idea at all.

3

As Mika drove up the winding road further into the mountains, I thought of the episodes of *Southern Justice* that my ex-husband loved to watch. Those officers had been driving into these hollows to stop fights or address folks who were drunk and disorderly, and there was always shouting and tears. I hoped we weren't making our way into the same.

While Mika drove, I looked up the Sutherlands' place on the county GIS site, and it looked to be pretty near the top, where the views were prettiest. But on a road like this that hadn't been bought out with people whose wealth afforded them not only the view but also the wherewithal to build, the living was hard. Historically, people had moved far up into the mountains so they could be left alone. Often that desire had been fueled by persecution because of people's ethnicity or nationality, but sometimes it had been driven by a desire to have the privacy needed for more questionable choices. I mean, I liked good apple pie moonshine as much as Mika, but, at least historically, the folks who brewed it weren't always the most friendly.

We pulled up to the Sutherland house, and I admired the red twig dogwoods planted in beds around the most lovely red maples. Growing up the daughter of a man who loved plants, especially when they were planted with an eye to the setting where they thrived, had made me appreciate a good landscaping job. Someone in the Sutherland house either had the knack for gorgeous plantings or had prioritized hiring someone who did. The yard was gorgeous down to the whimsical birdhouses that sat amongst the wild edges. I could tell songbirds loved this place, and I kind of wanted to live there myself.

As we pulled up, a short, white woman with brown hair curled around her soft, warm face stepped into the yard and dusted flour off her hands as she moved toward Mika's car. She wore an apron and clogs, and I felt an immediate desire to sit down at her kitchen table and drink hot tea while we shared our hard stories. The intensity of the morning was catching up to me, and I had to take a deep breath and bite my cheek to keep from tearing up when I stepped out of the car. Even through her gentle smile, I could see the pain in this woman's face.

Fortunately, Mika must have been thinking about what to say when we arrived while I searched the internet because as I stepped around the car, she said, "Mrs. Sutherland, we just met one of Rocket's friends, and we wanted to sit with you a bit if we could."

Mrs. Sutherland's forehead creased, but she stretched out her hand and said, "Oh, how kind of you. I'm Olivia."

"Mika, and this is Paisley. It's nice to meet you, but I wish it was under better circumstances." My best friend took the grieving mother's hand and held it in both of hers.

I stepped forward and smiled. "Peter Werzer told us that Rocket was a gifted climber. I bet he was at the top of these trees before he could even talk."

Olivia smiled. "That's why he got that nickname. One day I

came out here, and he was up in the top of that sycamore." She pointed to the large, white-barked tree that stood by the creek in front of the house. "He was three, and I thought I was going to have to get the fire department out to get him down."

"Did you do that thing where you stood under him and hoped you could at least break his fall?"

"Exactly. I knew if I went up there, he'd just go higher, so I just had to stand and watch him climb down. Nimble as a cat, that boy." She smiled at me. "I take it you know the type."

"My guy isn't quite three, so we haven't scaled massive trees yet, but bookshelves, scaffolding, fences. When he was eighteen months old, he climbed to the top of one of those huge swing sets at the park, and I ran around with my arms up in the air like I could somehow catch him when he tumbled from a story above me." I was getting a little anxious just remembering that day.

"Ah yes, braver than they are smart at that age," she said with a smile that quickly faded. "Maybe at any age." She looked past us toward the road briefly before giving her head a little shake and saying, "Please, where are my manners? Would you like to come in for some coffee? I just made a fresh pot."

There was not a cup of coffee I didn't like, and given the shock of the morning and my rising concern about my finances caused by this delay, I thought just what I needed was a mug of something warm in my hands. "That would be lovely."

We followed her through the door into a charming cottage. The walls were painted in soft shades of yellow and blue, and while there was some of the expected country décor – a rooster here, a collection of matching figurines there – the house was wonderfully bohemian with quilts and eclectic art hung on the walls. I stopped by a painting of a dark-skinned woman washing laundry in a river. The colors were rich, deep umbers and teal blues, and the posture of the woman was so powerful in how it showed both her strength and her exhaustion. It was the kind of simple art I loved because it told a story of a moment and a lifetime all in one.

Olivia came over to me and held out a hand-thrown pottery mug full of dark coffee. "I picked that one up in Madagascar a few years back when I went over with Doctors Without Borders. I relate to her. I expect you do, too." She looked at my ring finger. "Single mom?"

"Yep. And I do relate. It's beautiful." I took a sip of the coffee and felt a shiver of pleasure run down my spine. "This is delicious. Thank you. It's been a while since someone gave me something this delicious that I didn't have to pay for."

"Simple gifts," Olivia said as she turned to where Mika was admiring a collection of beach glass that was displayed in a shallow, earthenware bowl. "Like your visit. It's very kind of you to come by. Please sit."

Mika shot me a wide-eyed glance and then sat in a velvet-covered wingback chair that looked like a squatting hug. She was feeling uncomfortable about our false pretenses, and so was I.

I decided to come clean quickly and sat forward on the very comfortable sofa even though I wanted to sink back into the crazy quilt draped across its back. "Olivia, we really did want to come by and offer our sympathy over Rocket's disappearance, but—"

Olivia cut me off. "Paisley, you have lived in Octonia all your life, haven't you? You're Dale Sutton's girl, right?"

I nodded slowly.

"Well, then you know that news travels faster than a goose with a peanut around here. I already got the call about the body down the road, and I know the two of you found it. I appreciate you coming up here to talk to me, even if it's not just a social call." She held up the silver coffee pot she'd set on the table and looked at my mug.

I nodded again.

"Most folks would have just been gossiping about things at the Hoot and Scoot, but you women came right to me. I respect that." She sat back in a plush green chair-and-a-half and put her sock feet up on the ottoman. "So let's talk. I have no secrets."

Mika looked at me, and I widened my eyes. We both smiled and turned back to our host. "Well, do you think it could be Rocket they found?" Mika asked quietly.

Olivia sipped her coffee with quiet deliberation and then said, "It could be. At first, I thought he had just run off, taken flight to something bigger or at least shinier. But the longer time went on, the more frazzled Renee, his girlfriend, looked each time I saw her, the more I thought something might have happened to him."

I studied my coffee and said, "You thought Renee knew what happened to him?"

Olivia met my eyes. "I'm not sure I'd go that far. She has always been such a sweet girl, if a little willfully ignorant, but Rocket loved her and, therefore, so did I. They'd been together for years, and she spent more nights here than at home in the last couple of years Rocket was here. But after a couple months of him being gone, she'd skitter away from me every time she saw me at church or the grocery store."

"Could it have just been too painful for her to see you?" Mika asked.

"I've thought long and hard about that, and maybe, I guess. But more, she seemed scared, scared of what I'd say. Scared, maybe that I'd ask the wrong question." Olivia held the mug up under her nose and let the steam rise around her head.

I studied her face for a minute and said, "That's a very specific thing to think she'd be afraid of, isn't it?"

Olivia sighed. "I can see how it would sound that way to you, but if you'd seen the row Renee got into with her brother a couple nights before Rocket disappeared, you might have suspicions that you couldn't keep to yourself."

Mika and I shifted in our seats. "Do you want to tell us about what you saw?" I asked. I had been on God's green earth long enough to know that when people drop juicy tidbits like that, it's because they want you to gobble them down and ask for more.

Olivia leaned forward and put her mug on the coffee table between us. "I knew I liked you, Paisley. You too, Mika. You're not afraid to just ask what you need to ask."

"Some people say I'm nosy," I said with a small smile.

"Nosy is good in my book. Better than sly," Olivia said with a smile of her own as she settled back into her chair. "Renee and Rocket had been down at the movie theater in town seeing some old monster film, *The Mummy* maybe. They'd just come back, and we were all sitting on the porch enjoying the crisp air and the smell of the woodstove." She looked over at the black stove in the corner. "A truck pulled into the driveway, and Scott, Renee's brother, stepped out. He'd had a few too many, that was clear just from the way he tumbled out of the truck door, but since his truck was parked, I thought it better to make him welcome than to lecture him and send him back onto the roads."

I swallowed hard. This already sounded like a very hard story.

"He came stumbling up the front steps there and went to grab Renee. He said, 'You're coming home with me. You belong where I can keep an eye on you.'" Olivia's mouth twisted just a little as she talked. "I'd known Renee and Scott's mama and daddy for a long time. We all went to high school together. They were fine, but troubled, you know what I mean? Nothing obviously wrong, at least that I knew, but both of them made me a little uneasy. I know that's kind of a horrible thing to say, but it's the truth." Olivia grew silent.

I wanted to ask for their parents' names, but I knew there would be time for questions later. Now, I needed the story's momentum to carry Olivia on with the telling.

She took a ragged breath and said, "Rocket stood up and got between Renee and Scott, told that young man he needed to leave, that Renee could go if she wanted but he'd drive her home if that was the case."

"Renee didn't want to go, though?" Mika asked breathlessly.

"No, she did not. She was cowering in her chair, knees curled up to her chest and everything. That girl was terrified. But my son knows to respect a woman's wishes, and he would have taken her home if she wanted."

I felt myself growing shaky just at the thought of that moment. I'd been in too many situations with a man threatening me or threatening a friend of mine to not know a bit of how Renee felt.

"Renee finally found her voice," Olivia continued, "and said she was staying. Scott wouldn't back down though. He decided that if he couldn't bully his sister, he was going to take it out on Rocket. Fortunately, my boy's nickname may have come from his ability to climb fast, but it also meant he reacted fast. As soon as Scott took a swing, Rocket had him pinned to the ground. Twelve years of aikido had prepared him, and Scott didn't stand a chance. Rocket took his keys and then locked Scott in the guest room for the night."

"Wow, you let him stay here after that?" Mika's voice was squeaky with disbelief.

"It was either that, call the police, or let him drive home drunk. I decided to take the option that would keep the most people safe." She stared at the window. "I wonder, though, if it was that choice—"

This time I interrupted Olivia. "No, don't go there. You did a kind thing to protect a man who had just attempted to hurt your son. Do not take his possible actions onto your shoulders.

If he did something to Rocket, that's on him. Not on you." There was a strident edge to my voice, and I immediately wondered if I'd gone too far, had been too outspoken with a grieving woman who I'd just met.

When I looked at Mika, though, she was nodding. And when Olivia met my eyes, she had tears in them. "Thank you," she said. "I know that, you know. But hearing someone else say it . . ." She swallowed hard.

Mika stood and walked to the ottoman before sitting and taking Olivia's feet in her hands. Olivia looked down and then shifted into a more comfortable position. I admired these women who could give and take comfort so easily and wished I could do the same.

"Well, we don't know that the skeleton of the poor soul we found today is Rocket, and until we have an identification, let's assume your son is alive and well and enjoying life in a pocket of the world without telephones." Mika began to rub the arches of Olivia's feet, and our new friend sank with a soft groan deeper into her chair.

"But let me ask. Have you told Sheriff Shifflett about this encounter?" I said.

Olivia shook her head. "I didn't know if it was just overreaction or me seeking answers for something that doesn't have any answers. I didn't want to cast aspersions if they weren't warranted."

I smiled. "Well, I can tell you that the sheriff is very discreet and wouldn't accuse Scott of anything unless he had evidence to back it up."

"You know him personally then?"

Mika guffawed, and I saw a smile start to form on Olivia's face. "You know him well?"

I sighed. "We are, er, well, I'm not sure what we are, but I know he's a good person." I told her about the time the sheriff had taken Sawyer and me on a ride in his patrol car so that

Sawyer could see the sirens and lights in action. Saw talked about it almost every day still.

"He does sound like a good person." She stared at the window as Mika continued to massage her feet. It wasn't every person who would be comfortable and bold enough to rub the feet of a near-stranger, but then, my best friend wasn't every person. She had a very good sense of what people needed and how to best give it to them. Clearly, Olivia needed a little stress relief.

"He is a good person. And besides, it's been – how long has it been since Rocket went missing?"

"Eight years and three months."

I took a deep breath. "That's a long time to carry not knowing. Would you like me to call him, ask him to come now, while we're here with you?'

Olivia met my gaze and then a wry grin formed on her face. "But only if he brings some extra-cheese pizza and Dr. Pepper from Sal's. I need comfort food."

"We are going to be friends for life," I said as I took out my phone and stepped back out on the porch.

When the sheriff answered I said, "Santiago, I'm with Rocket Sutherland's mom. I think you're going to want to hear what she has to say."

There was a long silence on the other end of the line and then I heard a hard exhale. "Okay. I'm almost there."

I started to tell him about the pizza order, but then processed what he'd just said. "Wait, did you say you're almost here?"

"Yes, Paisley, I did." He sounded so very tired. "I need to do the notification. We identified the body you found as belonging to Stephen Sutherland, and I need to tell his mother."

. . .

In short order, I got the details from the sheriff and asked if I could tell Olivia. I felt I owed it to her, and I thought maybe it would be, somehow, a little easier to take from someone who was at least friend-ish if not an actual friend. Santiago agreed, asked me to finish telling him what pizza to bring, and to wait until he arrived, pizza in hand, to tell Olivia. I did remember to ask for what Olivia wanted, but I wasn't sure she was going to want food now.

I went back in the house and found myself both relieved and flustered that they were talking about yarn. It turned out that Olivia was an accomplished knitter, and they were bantering about stitches and yarn weights and such. I knew nothing about knitting – crochet was the only yarn-related thing I could do and only minimally – so I took the moment to prepare my thoughts. Unfortunately, that process required me to think about how I would want someone to tell me about Sawyer, and just that thought nearly ripped me open.

The knock at the door broke me out of my devastating reverie and reminded me I needed to tell Olivia that the sheriff was on his way, so I blurted, "The sheriff's here," with all the grace of a bulldog on a diving board and jumped up to answer the door.

Santiago gave me a sad smile and came in around me. "Mrs. Sutherland, I'm Santiago Shifflett."

Olivia stood and nodded. "I take it you don't have good news."

"No, ma'am, I don't." He looked at me, and I stepped forward to take Olivia's hands in mine.

"I asked the sheriff if I could tell you, Olivia. He needed to be here, first, though. I'm sure you understand." I was not sure of anything in that moment, but Olivia's dazed nod told me she at least was holding on to the rudiments of conversation by giving a response.

"They found a ring on the body," I said as my thumbs

rubbed back and forth across the knuckles of her hand. "A ruby class ring."

Olivia sat down abruptly. "Dad's ring." She stared at our joined hands for a minute, and I knelt down in front her. She met my eyes. "Stephen never took it off."

I felt Santiago step closer until his knees rested lightly against my shoulder blades. "Yes," he said. "Peter Werzer identified it."

Tears welled in Olivia's eyes, but she didn't break her eye contact with me. "I think I need you to say it."

I swallowed hard. "The body we found in the house down the road was Stephen's. I'm so sorry."

The keen that issued from Olivia's mouth was primal, and I felt it in my soul. Despite my earlier meditation on how I'd want to receive the news of my son's death, I had since been fighting hard not to think about Sawyer, not to imagine how I would feel in this moment, but that sound broke something open in me. I had to sit down, and I was glad that Santiago's legs and then his strong hands eased me to the ground. I looked up at him with gratitude.

Mika slid onto the ottoman beside Olivia, and the two of them rocked while I continued to hold Olivia's hands and cry along with her.

WE STAYED WITH HER, all three of us, until she could tell us who to call. She wanted to see Mary Johnson, a lifelong friend and a woman I had just begun getting to know myself. I couldn't think of a better person to be there in that moment. Mary had lost her son to cancer when he was a teenager, so if anyone understood the grief of losing a child, it was Mary.

I texted her quickly: *I'm at Olivia Sutherland's place. Can you come?*

Mary's response was almost instantaneous: *I'll be there in ten. It was Stephen then?*

Yes, was all I replied.

While Mika stayed close to Olivia, and Santiago went over what would need to happen next in order for Olivia to be able to have a funeral, I rummaged through her cabinets until I found her impressive stash of tea. I brewed us all a pot of honey chamomile and poured it into five mugs. Then, I found a box of Walker's shortbread and put that on a small plate. Shock was a hard thing, but sugar, old wives' tale or not, always helped.

As I came into the living room with my tray of sustenance, the front door eased open, and Mary stepped in. She must have done a hundred miles an hour to get up here from her house in town, but I knew Santiago would overlook the speeding for the sake of support.

Mary slid onto the ottoman on the other side of Olivia and wrapped her brown hands around her friend's cold, white ones. Then, Olivia started to cry again, deep, chest-racking sobs that I could feel in my own sternum.

Santiago, Mika, and I took our mugs and a cookie each and stepped onto the porch. "You did that very well, Paisley," Santiago said as he pulled me against him by slipping his arm around my waist. "Are you okay?"

"Comparatively, I am amazing. But still, the thought of Sawyer . . ."

Mika pulled me from Santiago's embrace and tugged my body to her chest. "Don't think about that. It will do you no good." She held me so tight that I could only think about my next breath, not when my son's breaths would stop. It was a gift.

When Mika finally let me go, I inhaled deeply and then stared out across the valley. The vineyard down below was beautiful with the white, bunched up bird net weaving across the dark brown vines, and it was nice to see tendrils of smoke coming up from people's woodstoves. The setting was really picturesque, but it felt selfish to enjoy it when Olivia's world had just finished falling apart.

The woman was stronger than I was, however, because just then, she and Mary came out to join us, and when Olivia saw the direction we were all facing, she said, "You see why we built up here, right? I never get tired of that view, and it never fails to remind me that no matter how terrible life is, beauty still rises up."

I turned to stare at this woman with her puffy eyes and enrapt expression and decided I was going to be more like her. "You have to hunt that beauty down, right?" I said more to myself than to anyone else.

"That's right. Beauty Hunters, that's what we are," Mary said as she wrapped her arm around her friend's shoulder. "Seek it and find it."

"Is that a verse about God?" Mika asked.

"Sure is. Don't see anything but God down there in that view," Olivia said quietly.

Santiago slipped his hand into mine and gave it a small squeeze. "Me either," he said.

4

Eventually, Mika and I made our way back down into town while Santiago got Olivia's statement about what had happened with Scott. We would have stayed if we were needed, but with Mary there, Olivia had good support, and I needed to get back to pick up Sawyer. I knew Dad and Lucille were probably getting tired, and Sawyer would be ready for some downtime, too. Plus, if Lucille was true to form, she and Saw had baked something amazing – last time it was banana bread cake with whipped frosting and pecan halves – and my son would be ready to come down from a sugar high in short order.

Plus, I really just needed to hug him for a long time.

Sure enough, when I got to Dad and Lucille's, Dad was taking his usual afternoon nap, and Lucille and Sawyer were in the process of cleaning the kitchen – which, it seemed, involved Lucille cleaning and Saw eating something that looked remarkably like Boston Cream Pie. "You made my favorite?" I asked as I walked into the kitchen.

Sawyer jumped up and ran to me with cream-covered

hands that became tiny cream handprints on the back of my pants. "We made your favorite."

"Thank you," I said, first to the top of my son's head and then to my stepmother. "Wow." Normally that word comes with a kick of enthusiasm, but I barely held my tears back as I said it.

Lucille gave my arm a squeeze, intuiting, I presumed, that any further sign of affection would lead to a breakdown, and said, "We actually made two of your favorites. One for here and now and one for you later." She opened the refrigerator door to show me the cake carrier all closed up and ready to go.

I smiled and swallowed as I said another thanks. "I need it."

Lucille winked. "I figured. And Sawyer was a great help. The here and now cake has just a little extra salt because Sawyer thought it important."

I winced. "Oh man."

"Yeah, you'll want a glass of water with that one," she said as she bent down to Sawyer's level and wiped a smudge of chocolate off his cheek. "Why don't you go wake up Boppy?"

My son loved a lot of things in life, but near the top of his list was the chance to wake someone up. His grandparents indulged him far better than I did, and so I sent him on his way and hoped that Dad had gotten a good rest already.

Lucille handed me a cup of peppermint tea and pointed to their back porch, which was cool but perfect for a moment of quiet conversation while the toddler was occupied. "You okay?" she asked.

I took a long sip of the tea and nodded. "I am. But Olivia Sutherland is not."

"So it was her son then?" Lucille asked with a slow shake of her head.

"Saul called Dad?"

"First thing. Wanted him to know since he figured you'd hear from the sheriff directly. Did Sheriff Shifflett tell you about Olivia?"

I sank down into the rocker and shook my head. "We were there, actually. Mika and me. Went up to talk to her before we even knew."

Lucille's eyes narrowed just a little. "You were snooping?"

"Not snooping. Being curious." I told Sawyer every day that being curious was a strong attribute in a human being, and I stood by that as baseline truth.

"Your father will not be pleased," she said, "but I am just outright curious myself. How did they ID the body? It's too quick for a DNA test."

I wrenched my head back on my neck. "How do you know that?"

"CSI," she said matter-of-factly. "And don't you go telling me that it's just TV. I like to live with my illusions, thank you very much."

I laughed. "Well, I do think in this case that's accurate. It was actually a ring that Rocket wore, one that belonged to his grandfather."

"Oh, wow. Well, that's not DNA, but that sounds pretty clear." Lucille frowned. "How did Olivia take it?"

I met my stepmother's gaze and held it. "It was awful and beautiful . . . and I can't really think about it anymore." I swallowed a huge lump in my throat.

Lucilled sipped her tea and let the silence linger just a minute before she said, "Maybe your father knew her father? How old is Olivia?"

I smiled. "About my age, maybe a few years older." It happened all the time – the mother of a young adult is the same age as me, with my toddler son. The number of times I got taken as Sawyer's grandmother almost outweighed the number of times people thought I was his nanny. It didn't seem to really register with people at playgrounds and in stores that a little boy calling a woman Mama might just be because she was, in fact, his mother.

"Well, let's ask him. Sawyer should have him good and awake by now," Lucille said with a wink.

We walked back inside and found Sawyer practicing his WWE moves on his prone grandfather. Fortunately, Dad and Lucille had learned, as had I, that it was best to curl in a ball with one's arms over one's head to withstand this onslaught. And we all took the beating because that little boy laughed the best laugh when he was playing wildly with his body.

But when I grabbed Sawyer around the middle and swung him away from his grandfather snoozing under the covers of his bed, I saw a flash of relief move across Dad's face before he sat up and said, "Boy, you are going to be the end of me," and grinned. "Now scoot so I can get some clothes on. I'm in my birthday suit."

"Let me see it," Saw said, and my dad blushed.

I wasn't a prude about nudity with Sawyer – I couldn't afford to be if I wanted to ever change clothes or bathe – but *I* didn't need to see all that, not today. Not any day. So I scooped Sawyer over my shoulder and jogged with him into the living room.

When Dad came out, thankfully clothed, I said, "Did you know Olivia Sutherland's dad?"

Dad blinked a few times and said, "You mean Lanky Sutherland?"

"His name was *Lanky*?" I asked.

"Well, not his given name, but the guy was tall and thin, like a walking rope." Dad rubbed a hand over his head. "Come to think of it, I'm not sure I know the name his mama gave him."

I rolled my eyes. Everyone around here had a nickname, including me, although I didn't like to think about it. When I was a teenager, I had terrible acne, and I also burned in the sun like an ant under a magnifying glass, so mean kids called me "Pocked and Pasty." It was awful. In comparison, "Lanky" was pretty tame.

"His daughter they called 'Dinky,' I think," Dad mused.

"Lanky and Dinky. I don't need to know where Dinky came from," I said as I suppressed the desire to roll my eyes again. "So you knew him then?"

"I did. I expect you're asking because it was actually his grandson you found?" Dad sat down hard in his seat on their sofa and stared at Sawyer, who was diligently connecting his magnetic train set.

I nodded and watched my dad study his one and only grandson. "He had on his grandfather's ring," I said.

Dad studied Sawyer a minute more and then went back into his room only to return a moment later. "Look like this?"

I took the gold ring from his hand and studied it. "I'm not sure. I didn't see it, but is this your class ring?" It was small, more the size of today's class rings for women, not the massive, knuckle busters that, at least when I was in high school, the guys wore.

"It is," Dad said. "I've never worn it, but your grandmother insisted I get one. She was so proud I graduated, even prouder I went on to college."

Dad had grown up the child of tobacco sharecroppers in the eastern part of Virginia, and he and his brother were the first in their family to go to college. Dad went on and got a master's, too, but he'd never forgotten his roots, the hard toil it took for his parents just to keep him alive, much less help him thrive.

"She really loved you." I thought back to Olivia, that keening cry, and then cleared my mind of the memory. It was too painful. "Did you know any Morrises back then?" The question slipped out before I thought, but it was too late to pull it back because Dad was already laughing.

"Paisley, girl, how many Morrises did you go to school with? Twenty? Thirty? We had at least that many back in my day. You can't throw a stick out here without hitting a Morris or a Shifflett, you know that. Care to be more specific?"

I sighed. "I don't know their grandparents' names, but the grandkids are Renee and Scott Morris."

Dad frowned and grunted just a little. "Preacher Morris's kids?"

I shrugged. "I have no idea if their dad is a preacher or not."

"No, his name is Preacher, his nickname anyway. That Scott Morris drives a big pickup, all lifted and gaudy with stickers."

I thought about the way Olivia had described Scott's truck and nodded. "Yeah, I think that's him."

"You stay away from those people, Paisley," Dad said as he stood up. "They are no good. No good at all."

Lucille stepped into the room. "Dale Sutton, I have not ever heard you talk so ugly about anyone. What did those people ever do to you?"

Dad grunted again and walked out the back door.

I looked at Lucille with befuddlement. She was right. Dad never talked bad about anyone, even if they deserved it. But he was mad now, mad and scared, and now I needed to know what he knew. Maybe it would help find Rocket's killer.

"You go," she said. "I'll talk to him later. I've got this guy." She sat down on the floor and stretched out her legs so Sawyer could run his trains up and down them like tracks.

"I'll be right back, Love Bug. We'll get french fries and a milkshake on the way home." Sawyer smiled up at me and went right back to his trains, but I knew he wasn't going to forget that promise. Neither was I because I didn't have the energy to cook, and I really wanted that double cheeseburger on the value menu for myself.

When I walked into the backyard, I had to do a quick circuit to find Dad, but eventually I saw him at the back of their lot. He was building a bonfire to burn up the fallen sticks and ivy clippings he'd gathered. Dad always built fires when he needed an excuse to be outside and away from people. I was going to give him his space, but only after he told me what he knew.

I pulled up a five-gallon bucket and sat down, watching the fire grow under my dad's expert tending. "Dad, it's possible that Scott Morris is involved in Stephen Sutherland's death. I need to know what you know. Please." I spoke softly but right by my dad's good ear, and I knew he heard me. But I also knew my father would only speak when he was ready.

Fortunately for my butt and my hunger, I didn't have to wait long before Dad started talking in a low murmur. "When you were a baby, I watched Preacher Morris smack his wife across her mouth at the gas station."

I gasped but let Dad continue. "I'm not sure he knew anyone else was there since it was late at night, but I also don't think he cared much. But I cared a lot and told him so. Offered to give his wife a ride home, but she wouldn't take it."

I shifted on the bucket.

"Kept an eye on him after that, and while I never saw him lay a hand on her again, she came up with black eyes and broken arms a fair amount. Then, I saw that little blonde boy following around after him like he was the greatest thing on God's green earth." Dad's voice broke. "I couldn't do a thing, and now you're asking after that little boy . . ."

I stared into the fire for a moment. "Yeah, I am," I said. "He threatened Rocket Sutherland a few nights before Rocket died." I didn't feel like it was helpful to say that Scott had been treating his sister like Preacher had treated their mom, but I did say, "I think it's safe to say the son learned from the father."

Dad shook his head. "They always do." He tossed another log on the slow-burning fire, and I patted his shoulder as I walked back into the house. I needed to tell Santiago what Dad had told me, but it would have to wait until after Sawyer was in bed. I needed time with my son, quality time . . . with fast food.

. . .

After Sawyer was filled up with chicken nuggets and I'd finished his "pink" milkshake, bedtime was smooth and easy. A tired toddler is a wonderful toddler, as long as he didn't go over the tipping point into overtired. By some great grace, I managed to time lights out just right, and he was asleep quickly. It had been a long day, and I needed some extended time to process what had happened.

I had just gotten out my latest journal – a spiral-bound, college-ruled notebook that I'd picked up at the dollar store because I couldn't afford the fancy journals I loved so much – and was going to write out the day's events when I got a text.

Santiago: *In the area, have time for a chat on the porch? I'll bring hot cocoa and whiskey.*

Me: *Ten minutes.*

Santiago: *Make it five. I'm pulling in now.*

I grinned. I'd missed our porch chats, but I had been the one to ask for space, to tell the sheriff I wasn't sure I was ready. After today, though, I needed to talk, and I needed to talk to someone who I didn't have to get up to speed first. My journal was my third best choice, and Mika my second. But my best friend processed hard things differently than I did, and I knew she wouldn't be ready to talk about Rocket Sutherland until at least tomorrow, maybe the next day.

So the chance to talk with the sheriff, to get more information about the case, and to spend time with a man I liked more and more each time I saw him, well, that choice was my ideal. I gathered up the lap blankets I kept in a basket for just such occasions and headed out to unfold the camp chairs and prop the front door open so I could hear if Sawyer came down the stairs.

Santiago came around the house just as I was sitting, and he handed me a plastic mug and filled it with hot chocolate. Then, he took two small bottles, like the ones from hotel room bars, and poured one each into our mugs. Only then did he sit and say, "Hi, Paisley."

I blushed just from the way he said my name, soft and round, like a late-blooming flower. "Hi, Santiago," I said in an almost-whisper. "Thank you for this. Thank you for coming."

"No need to thank me. I needed good company tonight. It's been a long day." He sipped from his mug. "For you, too."

I sighed. "Everything okay after we left Olivia's? I felt bad that we didn't stay."

He reached over and touched my hand gently. "I know, but it was good you left. Olivia said over and over again that she appreciated you being there, but she's one of those people, I think, who can't really do what she needs to do until she's alone. She told me about the altercation with Scott Morris, and I left. I wasn't there much longer than you were."

"Mary stayed, though, right?" I was like what Santiago described; I needed a lot of time alone to deal with regular life. But I knew that if I had just found out my son was dead, I would need someone there.

"She did. She was in the kitchen making chicken noodle soup when I left. She was going to sleep on the couch and stay as many days as Olivia needed." Santiago squeezed my fingers. "Olivia will be okay."

I sighed. "I know. But I can't imagine." I stared out across the field below my house. "Actually, that's a lie. I can imagine, and that's the problem." I gave my head a little shake and forced myself to think about something else. "I know you can't tell me anything about the case, but maybe you can tell me if the information that Olivia gave you about Scott Morris was useful." I really, really didn't want to pry, but I also didn't want to tell tales about someone and share what Dad had told me unless there was valid reason. This Scott guy was a total cretin, no doubt, but there were lots of horrible people in the world, and most of them didn't commit murder.

"It was . . . And thank you for knowing I can't tell you more." I could feel the sheriff's eyes on my face.

"Okay, then, but I can tell you." I relayed what Dad had shared that afternoon, and Santiago nodded.

"I've heard similar stories, and I'm looking at patterns. For this . . . for more." Santiago said quietly. "I'm watching, Paisley. I'm keeping an eye on him."

I took a long sip of my hot cocoa and felt the warmth all the way to my toes. I didn't normally drink hard liquor, but I might just have to indulge this way a bit more often. "Okay, I'm glad. I won't ask more." It was hard for me not to probe, not just to ask around the edges of the investigation to see what Santiago could and would tell me, but I knew that pushing too hard would compromise his position as sheriff . . . and doing that would compromise him and whatever it was we were building here on this cold night.

"I appreciate that," he said. "Now, a question for you. How much deeper into winter do you think we can tolerate the front porch? Because—"He lifted his legs and kicked his feet just a bit. "I do believe my toes have gone numb."

I laughed. "You sure that's not the whiskey?"

"No," he answered instantly, "I'm pretty sure it's the cold."

I smiled and stood. "My couch is your couch." I held the front door open and followed him into the living room, where Beauregard was already prone in front of the gas fireplace. If I hadn't been expecting to see him there, I might have thought that someone had tossed a large, misshapen throw pillow into the middle of the floor. When he heard us walk in, he stretched and, as best I could tell, intentionally placed one part of his body across every conceivable walking path into the room. For the first time, I realized why people were willing to own bigger houses despite the extra cleaning and expense involved. It must be because a grumpy Maine Coon was a trip hazard in any normal-sized house.

I used my foot to nudge Beau out of the way and let Santiago take a seat on the couch before I sat at the other end. My couch was a love seat, so the "other end" was really about six inches away, but I did my best to stay on my cushion entirely.

Santiago leaned forward and picked up my embroidery hoop. "I knew you cross-stitched, but I didn't realize you did such intricate work. Is this linen?"

I leaned back and looked at him carefully. "It is, but you are literally the first person ever to note that. Well, except for the FlossTube folks on Instagram. They can spot 32-count linen from space."

"What? You think a small-town sheriff doesn't know his fabrics?" He smiled out of the corner of his mouth. "I'll have you know that my mother is an avid stitcher herself. And I've even been known to pick up thread and make an *x* or two from time to time."

"You cross-stitch?" I asked and then immediately regretted my judgmental tone. "I'm sorry. I think that's great, but it's just that cross-stitchers have a sort of reputation—"

"For being little old white ladies with lots of cats." He glanced at Beauregard and then back at me. "I know. My mom is one of those ladies."

I blushed. "So you think I'm old?" I said and was surprised at how much emotion came out with my words.

"Not a bit. But you do have enough cat there to count for four of the creatures, so you're well on your way to living into the stereotype." He winked at me. "I haven't sewn in a long time, but when I was little and Dad worked second shift, Mom and I spent a lot of evenings just the two of us. She wanted to be able to do her hobby without feeling like she was leaving me out, I guess, so she got me a little hoop and a teddy bear kit."

I sighed. "I've been thinking I'd like to teach Saw for the

same reason. I love the idea of you and your mom sitting there sewing together."

"And I love the idea of you and Sawyer doing the same." He glanced back at the beige fabric still in his hand. "But maybe start him with something simpler, 14-count Aida."

"Good plan." I put out my hand and accepted the hoop when he handed it to me. I looked down at the small cluster of stitches that I'd just begun the night before. It was going to be an elaborate winter scene with a red bank barn set behind a split rail fence and a snow-covered tree. I'd bought the pattern a few years earlier because I just loved the simplicity of the colors and figured it would be something my dad might like to hang in his house. Last night, I'd decided to start stitching it in honor of the new salvage I was starting. "I just started it. Now, I think I'll stitch it and think of Rocket, of Olivia."

"Like a prayer shawl," Santiago said with a nod.

I tilted my head and looked at him wide-eyed. "First he identifies linen, and now he knows about prayer shawls. Next you're going to tell me that you knit hats for newborns in the UVA NICU."

"Nope," he said as he held his calloused hands in front of me, "baby-weight yarn just gets snagged on these claws. But I do drop off the hats my abuela and her friends knit and crochet once a month."

I stared at him and then gave my head a little shake before pulling my needle free from the fabric and saying, "Do you mind? It helps me think and calms me to sew."

"I don't mind at all." He peered down into the jumble of thread bobbins, needle pouches, and pencils that lived in my sewing basket. "It soothes me to put things in order, so would you be offended if I . . .?"

"You want to organize my sewing basket? Please do." I gestured toward the cabinet on the wall behind him. "That's where most of my thread is . . . all the bobbins are in order by DMC number. Go crazy."

He smiled and began to sort things into piles. I folded my legs under me and began to sew. We sat that way for another hour, me stitching, him sorting, and more than once I thought, *Well, I could get used to this.*

5

The next morning, Sawyer woke me with a gentle slap on the face. He was really being sweet, but no pat on my head at six forty-five feels tender. Fortunately, I managed to smile and say, "Good morning, Love Bug. Don't you want to come lay down just a little while longer?" instead of swearing.

Unfortunately, no matter how much I hoped, my little boy did not go back to bed once he was up. Sometimes, I could convince him to lay beside Beauregard at the foot of the bed, and I'd grab a few more minutes. But typically, the cost of this ploy – Beau's haughtiness and sometimes horribly placed hairballs – were not worth the three-and-a-half extra minutes of shut-eye. Beau loved Sawyer, but from a distance, and, before dawn, I felt much the same.

Still, I forced my eyes open, stood up, and got my slippers on before a tiny head barreled into my thigh and said, "Come on, Mama, let's go downstairs."

I thudded my way down the stairs as Sawyer bounced ahead of me, and when he dropped onto the couch with his toy excavator, I made my way into the kitchen to start the coffee.

For the first time in my life, I wasn't using an electric coffee maker but a French press, and I couldn't say I hated it. It was faster and more energy-efficient, and I also thought the coffee was better, richer. Honestly, though, most mornings, I would have been quite satisfied with fast food coffee or a caffeine IV.

The kettle on and the coffee grounds scooped, I headed back in and sat next to my son. Fortunately, I had managed to tuck my now perfectly organized sewing basket back into its cabinet the night before, so it was safe and sound (at least until Sawyer found the hiding spot). He was a bit young and busy for sewing lessons just yet, so, instead, I settled for watching his favorite young singer perform on *America's Got Talent*. He could watch that little girl sing the same song over and over again all day. She was a powerhouse. I had to give him credit for good taste.

Our quiet moments were short-lived, however, because the sun was streaming through the farmhouse windows and Sawyer was itching to get out there. I downed my first mug of coffee while I got him into his clothes. He didn't even protest because I promised him some time at the playground first thing. Then, I skittered upstairs to don my own layers of warmth to stave off the chilly temperatures while I did a little research from a park bench near the slides.

A travel mug of coffee and a toddler who only deigned to wear a jacket on threat of staying home made up my entourage as we loaded into the car for a drive over to the county park. This early in the day, only other toddlers would be there, and by silent agreement the other parents and I would sit quietly in our own corners and enjoy some quiet time while being sure no one in our line of sight broke an arm. There is really nothing quite like never being alone while also not being able to carry on a real conversation with the person constantly in your presence. It was one of the hardest things about single parenting for me.

Only one other family was there, a woman and a man and a little girl. I presumed the man and woman were the little girl's parents, but given my experience with being labeled Sawyer's grandmother far too often, I did my best not to assume anything about how those three people were connected.

The girl looked to be about Sawyer's age with two blonde pigtails sticking up above her rosy-cheeked face. She was dressed in so much baby pink that I wondered if her parents had simply opted for a single-color for her wardrobe in the hopes of ease. Baby pink was not my favorite color, but I had to admit that the hue looked really nice against her ivory skin. She was truly adorable.

Sawyer took to her immediately and invited her to do everything with him – climb the two-story climbing wall, descend the rope ladder, slide on the twisty slide. The little girl shook her head every time, and I didn't blame her. She climbed well for a toddler, very well, but compared to my son, she seemed behind. This was the curse of Sawyer's physical precociousness – other kids his age just couldn't do what he did, and older kids wanted to play more complex games than he was able to mentally grasp. So he often played alone and just watched the other children. My heart broke for him a little, but I knew it would all level out in time. His body would slow down, and his brain would catch up. Meanwhile, he'd learn how to manage difference, and that wasn't a bad thing at all.

Eventually, he and the little girl settled into a quiet game of piling up rubber chunks from beneath the monkey bars, and Sawyer seemed quite happy. Eventually, the woman who was with the little girl came over and said, "They're pretty cute, huh?"

I smiled up at her and scooted over so she could sit. "They are," I said as she settled onto the bench next to me. "That's my son, Sawyer."

"He's adorable, and he can really climb," she said.

"Tell me about it," I replied. "More than once I've pondered which is worse – him breaking an arm or the one I'll get trying to catch him."

"Wow. Nadia there doesn't really do climbing. She's much more of a 'read books to her dolls' kind of girl," she said.

"My kind of woman," I said. "I'm Paisley."

"Yes, we know who you are," the man who'd been with the woman said from just behind my head. "Paisley Sutton." His voice was tight with something that sounded a lot like anger.

I didn't like him behind me like that, so I stood up and faced him and the woman, who stayed on the bench and looked mortified. "Do I know you?" I said and glanced behind me to be sure Sawyer was still where I'd last seen him. He was, and I quickly calculated how I could grab him and get to the car if need be. This guy was giving me the creeps.

He was tall, over six feet, and wore a camo baseball cap low down over his eyes. The skin beneath his dark stubble looked sweaty, like he'd just come in from a run. "No, you don't know me, but I heard talk that you've heard of me."

The woman stood up and stepped toward me. At first, I thought she was moving to defend me, but then I noticed she stood just a bit behind me, putting me between her and the man. "Stop it, Scott," she said quietly.

I froze and took a quick breath, but fortunately, Scott was glaring at the woman and didn't notice. "I'm sorry, Scott. I don't think I do know you. Help me out?" I'd learned from experience that playing dumb was the best course of action when it came to men who liked to bully.

"You're going to act like you didn't sic the sheriff on me this morning?" He stepped from around the bench, and the woman and I both took a step back.

Another quick glance back told me that Sawyer had noticed the situation and was coming this way. I reached a hand back and felt his fingers grab mine.

"I really don't know what you're talking about." This time, my confusion was very real. It was pretty early, not even nine, so I was surprised that Santiago had already talked to Scott . . . but more, I knew that Santiago would never tell Scott anything about me, not for any reason, but especially not if the guy was dangerous. And there was no doubt, this guy was dangerous.

"Rocket's mom called my sister there to tell her about the sheriff coming. Wanted us to be prepared, right, Renee?" He took another step forward, and the four of us – Nadia was now in her mother's arms – stepped back again.

"That's right, Scott. When you heard me talking to Olivia, it was because Olivia wanted both of us to know the sheriff was coming. That's why I suggested we come here, to get some quiet and privacy." Renee was speaking calmly and evenly, but her eyes kept flicking over to me. She wanted me to understand, and I did. She was warning me, telling me to keep up her story.

"Oh, you were Rocket's girlfriend, Renee," I said as casually as I could. "It's so nice to meet you. And you must be her brother, Scott. Nice to meet you, too." My experience of life had also taught me that bullies can often be easily flattered.

Scott did seem to draw back a bit, or at least the menacing energy that was flying off him reined in a little.

"Yeah, we were there when the sheriff gave Olivia the news about Rocket's body yesterday," I said. "I'm sorry to you both. You were all so close, and I know it must have been hard to hear about your friend being mu—dead." I didn't think it wise to bring up murder here, and I was glad I caught myself.

Scott harrumphed, but then he turned away and said, "Yeah, sad news." He didn't sound sincere, but I'd take anything that distracted him.

I cut my eyes to Renee quickly, and she nodded. "That's right. We were all close. Olivia didn't say, but maybe you know." Her eyes widened as if begging me to understand again. "The sheriff wanted to talk to us because he was hoping we might be able to give him some information that would help him understand how Stephen died, that right?"

I swallowed hard. "Yep, I expect that's it exactly. No one is sure what happened and why Rocket ended up in that house." I knew it was a little risky to reveal where the body had been found, but I figured that the news had already traveled out so it was worth the risk if I sounded credible. "I bet the sheriff just hoped two of his closest friends could shed some light on things."

By this time, Scott looked bored and was far more tilty on his feet. The flask he pulled out of his back pocket told me all I needed to know about where that wobble was coming from and about what we needed to do. We needed a way out, and fast . . . for all four of us.

I scouted about, but there was no one else around. My car was a good fifty feet away, and while Renee and Scott's was closer, I was willing to bet she didn't have the keys. I was just about to slide my hand into my pocket and dial nine-one-one for help when Scott said, "I have to pee," and wandered toward the concession stand on the other side of the playground from us.

"We'll have to risk it. Let's go," I said to Renee, and without another word, the four of us flew into my car, Renee in the back with the two kids, and me in the front, and we sped out of the parking lot before Scott could even get his fly up.

I drove as quickly and as carefully as I could since the children weren't in their car seats. Fortunately, Sawyer thought it all a big game and cheered the whole time. Nadia and Renee looked terrified, but I couldn't blame them. Renee, though, kept her wits about her and said, "The child locks are on back here, right?"

I nodded as I reached over and locked the window controls, too. "The sheriff is a friend. I'm going to his office. We'll park out back in the lot with the cruisers. They'll keep us safe."

Renee nodded, and I made my way, with as much speed as I safely could muster, the five minutes into town.

Renee and I shuffled the stunned children into the station, and the dispatcher took one look at us and called the sheriff. "Sheriff, we need you out here, right now," he said.

Santiago strode out of his office, saw me, and pointed to his office door. The four of us made our way in, and I heard him tell the dispatcher, "We need chocolate milk and coffee . . . and find some markers and paper."

Despite the adrenaline coursing through me, I smiled. He always knew just what to do.

Renee and I each took a seat and pulled our toddlers close. I reached over and put my hand over hers, but she didn't respond. From the way all the blood had left her face, I figured she was doing everything she could to keep it together for Nadia. I'd had those moments – although not quite this scary – and I knew how important it was for her to stay calm with her daughter nearby.

Santiago sat on the top of his desk and looked at the four of us closely. Sawyer was staring at the edge of the desk, and Santiago gently knelt down and put his face in Saw's line of vision. "Hi Sawyer. It's good to see you. Your mom and her friend are going to talk to me now. Is that okay?"

My son broke out of his stare long enough to give a little nod, and then Santiago turned to Nadia. "Hi, Little Lady. I'm Sheriff Shifflett. Is it okay with you if your mommy—" He looked up at Renee, who nodded. "—if your mommy tells me your name?"

Nadia gave the tiniest nod possible then buried her face in Renee's chest. "Her name is Nadia, and I'm Renee. Renee Morris." Her voice was steady but very soft, and again, I got the impression she was holding on by a thread.

"Would you like to tell me what happened, or do we need to

wait a little while, get everyone settled, maybe get Ms. Mika to come down?" Santiago said as he held my gaze.

"I heard you ask for chocolate milk," I said, feeling my body begin to tremble as the adrenaline surge left my muscles. "We might all need some of that, and yes, let's call Mika. Maybe we could all go to her store and let the kids play while we talk." I nodded slowly to Santiago, knowing he would understand that we didn't want to scare the children further.

"I love that idea. Let me check on that chocolate milk, and I'll be right back." He put his hand quickly on my shoulder as he left, and I turned to Renee again. She still looked terrified, but at least some color was beginning to come back into her cheeks.

Sawyer slid down to the floor and from some reserve of toys and strength pulled out a tiny firetruck and began to scoot it around the chair legs. Nadia caught sight of the game and eventually climbed down beside him.

By the time Santiago returned, both kids were making truck noises and clambering around on his desk and chair. The sheriff smiled and said, "Glad they're feeling a little better." He looked at me and a wrinkle formed between his eyes for just a moment before he turned to the children. "Who wants chocolate milk?"

Two tiny faces looked up and smiled, and Santiago gave them small miracles in the form of sippy cups full of thick, sweet milk. Then, he handed two mugs of what turned out to be hot cocoa to Renee and me and said, "I figured you needed the warmth and the sugar. Take your time. Mika will be ready for us when we get there."

I nodded and mouthed thank-you before letting the trembles travel through my arms. Next to me, Renee clutched her mug with both hands but drank steadily. A little warmth and a little sugar went a long way.

. . .

A FEW MINUTES LATER, we moved back through the station, Renee with Nadia on her hip and Sawyer holding Santiago's hand. I had thought we'd walk the couple blocks up the street, but Santiago proved wiser than I was and had parked his cruiser right by the front door. He strapped the kids into the two cars seats he'd borrowed from the department's stock for emergencies and then asked Renee and I if we could tolerate close quarters up front with him for the short ride. "If not, Officer Winslow can follow us in another car with one or both of you."

I could see the beginnings of panic on Renee's face and quickly said, "We'll snuggle. No problem. I'll get in the middle."

Renee climbed silently in next to me, and then we were off with the lights on and the sirens going as we drove twenty-five miles an hour down Main Street. Nadia and Sawyer were laughing with delight, but the show was setting Renee on edge a bit. I reached over and took her hand and said, "Almost there."

"He's going to know where we are," she whispered.

"I've taken steps," Santiago said quietly. "Officers are in place. You will be safe, and we have a plan for when you leave." He parked the car in front of Mika's shop and then looked Renee in the eye. "You are safe."

She sighed and nodded, and then we stepped out and were met by not only Mika but Dad and Lucille, too. They got the kids out of their car seats and then let Renee guide Nadia into the yarn shop. What I saw there amazed me. Somehow, in the past fifteen minutes, they had constructed an entire maze from cardboard boxes. It ran most of the length of the floor and featured doors of every size and shape. Sawyer was inside it as soon as his grandfather gave him permission, and with a nod from Renee, Nadia followed suit.

Lucille put both her hands on Renee's shoulders and said, "We will take good care of your girl." Then, she turned Renee to the back of the store. "That woman there, that's Officer Winslow. She's armed and ready. You're safe."

I looked back at the deputy in her jogging suit and nodded. She smiled and turned her attention back to the store, keeping an eye on both exits.

Mika led Renee and me to her wingback chairs, which were now positioned in the center of the store instead of in their usual place by the front window. A tall shelf full of baskets of yarn stood between the front of the store and us. It was an unobtrusive but very effective screen, and I was confident that neither Scott nor anyone else could see us or the kids. We really were safe, especially since I could see another police car parked behind Santiago's and an officer in the front seat.

"How did you know?" I asked first thing. Obviously someone had tipped Santiago off to what had happened. Otherwise, he wouldn't have known to guard us so carefully.

"Someone was walking their dog in the park and saw the interaction with Scott. They lingered because it looked iffy to them and they thought they might need to release their mastiff to scare Scott off if need be." Santiago smiled. He apparently liked this citizen's idea of assistance. "But when they saw you bolt for the car, they knew the situation was serious and called us right away. I hoped you'd come to the station, so I waited. If you hadn't made it there quickly, I was going to call you and find out where you'd gone. We were ready to mobilize." He gave Renee a long look.

"Thank you," I said and saw Renee nod beside me.

"Are you two okay? I mean beyond being traumatized and terrified?" the sheriff asked.

"Yes, I think so. Are you okay, Renee?" I hadn't noticed any bruises or anything to indicate she'd been assaulted physically, but I knew there were ways to hide bruises and that it didn't have to be physical to be abuse.

"Yes." Her voice was thin. "I'm okay, and Nadia's okay. It was a scary morning though."

"I'm so sorry I put you in danger with my phone call, Renee. I really didn't think it would set Scott off, not that quickly." Santiago said as he leaned forward just a little to catch Renee's eye.

Renee nodded. "Why would you? It was just a call to get information. I told Scott that, but he is so suspicious, so convinced that everyone is out to get him."

I sighed. "Does he have something to hide?"

Renee shrugged. "I really don't know. But when he acts like that, it makes me think he does, you know?"

"We'll get the information we need from him soon, Renee, and we'll keep you safe while we do. But first, can you tell me what happened this morning? What led you to go to the park?"

Renee ran her fingers down her neck and out of nowhere, Mika appeared with a bottle of water, which Renee took with a small smile. After she took a long pull of the water, she said, "After you called, Scott was storming around the house and throwing things. Talking about how everyone was out to get him for something he didn't do. That just because he was protecting his little sister that day everyone thought he killed Stephen. He was so furious." Tears pooled in Renee's eyes.

I looked at Santiago, and he took a deep breath. "So you thought it might be good to get out of the house, is that right?"

Renee focused on the sheriff again. "Yes, exactly. He was terrifying Nadia, so I told him that I was taking her to the park. But he wouldn't let us go alone. Said he thought we'd run off and leave him. I had been thinking I'd go away for a while, but he insisted on driving, even though he doesn't have a car seat in his truck."

I saw Santiago make a mental note of that before he said, "And that's when you saw Paisley and Sawyer there?"

Renee swallowed hard and said, "Yes, I'm so sorry. I thought if I came over and talked to you I might be able to convince Scott that you didn't accuse him of anything. I'd made the mistake of telling Scott that you had mentioned his name as someone who knew Stephen. I'm so sorry I got you into all of this."

"Please," I said, "you didn't do anything wrong. None of us did, okay? Your brother has some, um, issues, and those are his to deal with. I'm glad I was there, actually. Glad we could get away like we did."

Renee smiled. "I have to admit I would have liked to see Scott's face if that huge dog had charged him."

I laughed. "Me, too."

While the kids tunneled to the center of the earth with Baba and Boppy chasing them and Auntie Mika plying them with cookies, Santiago began to question Renee about Rocket's death. At first, she was slow to talk, but as she began to remember, the words seemed to spill out as if a logjam in a stream had broken free finally.

Renee said that she and Stephen had been really happy. She was hoping he was going to propose, but then Scott seemed to go kind of crazy. "It was kind of out of nowhere," she said. "He just started talking about how I was tarnishing my reputation and giving people the wrong impression of me." Apparently, this kind of talk had gotten worse and worse over a couple of months.

But it all came to a head in the days just before Rocket was killed. "It was horrible. Scott wouldn't let me out of the house, said I was defiling myself with that man. For three days he kept me locked up until one night after he passed out, I climbed out the bedroom window and ran to my best friend's house."

Santiago took down the name of her friend, and I recognized her last name as belonging to a really generous family in Octonia. I made a note to write a story about their family history in one of my newsletters, a sort of quiet tribute to their generosity.

"Did Scott use the word *defiled*?" I asked when my train of thought returned to the station we were in. "I only ask because that sounds like something really old-fashioned."

"I know, right?" Renee said. "It was a word he picked up from that church up in Pig Hollow, you know the one where they make the women all wear dresses and work themselves to death for their men?"

Santiago's expression darkened. "Mountain Green Church, you mean?"

Renee nodded. "Yep, that's the one. Scott had been going there for a while back about the time Stephen disappeared. I don't know what he saw in those people, especially in that pastor. All they did was make him feel bad about himself, and when Scott is down on himself he drinks."

I shuddered. "And I expect the more he drank the more they came down on him, right?" I asked. I knew the type of group that did that – bully people into feeling horrible and then bully them some more when they do anything to dull the pain caused by the bullying.

"Yep. Finally, he stopped going, but only because Stephen convinced him that those people didn't care about him. He helped Scott see that we actually cared about him and loved him no matter what." Renee sighed. "It didn't last long, though, but it was a good couple of weeks. Scott was happy and had stopped drinking. He had started to do some work for some construction company, and he was happy. But that all ended the night he came to the Sutherland's place. He was back to that controlling BS, and I knew I couldn't take it anymore." Renee sunk back into her chair.

"How long after that did Rocket go missing?" Santiago asked.

"Three days." Renee's voice was flat.

There were a million things that Santiago could have asked then, things about what Renee thought had happened or if she'd seen her brother do anything suspicious, but he didn't ask. Instead, he stayed with what Renee actually knew.

"If you don't mind me asking, Ms. Morris, how did you end up back living with your brother?" Santiago's tone was kind. He wasn't judging, just trying to understand.

"Things were hard after Stephen died. I got in with some people who didn't really care about me, and I made a mistake, just the kind of mistake that Scott had thought I was making with Stephen. I got pregnant, and the guy didn't want to have any part of it. I couldn't afford my rent and a baby, and so I had to move home. Scott said he was happy to have us both, but . . ." She didn't finish her thought, and she didn't need to.

I turned to watch my son crawl around on the floor and forced myself to notice his chubby cheeks in an effort to not lose my temper.

"Well, you don't have to go back there again. If you're willing, Lucille has a place you can go. It's not too far from here, and they can help you and Nadia get set up in your own place once you're back on your feet," the sheriff said as he looked up and caught Lucille's attention.

She came over, and I stood to give her my seat. She leaned in and took Renee's hand and began telling her about the shelter down in town where she volunteered. It was a good place, a place Renee and Nadia would be safe and would get the support they needed as they started over.

Santiago bounced his head toward the front of the store. We walked toward the door, and he said, "Now, really, are you okay?"

I sighed. "I am. But that man almost had a mama and a dog at his throat this morning. Coming at me with my son there." My fear was fading back to let the rage come forward.

Santiago rubbed my arm. "I know. But you did exactly the

right thing. I'm so glad you came here. The idea of having to find you with that angry man looking for you, too . . ." He swallowed hard.

"You were the first safe place I thought of," I said quietly and then let myself briefly fall against his chest as he pulled me close and stroked my hair.

After a few deep breaths, I stood up straighter and said, "You do have people out looking for Scott Morris, right?"

"Looking?!He's already at the station in a cell! We can hold him for assault using the witness's testimony, and now that I know he drives around with an unsecured child in his car, we've got him for even more."

All the moisture left my throat. "But I did that, too, with two children."

"The law makes exceptions for situations of extreme danger. I won't have to book you today, Paisley," he said with a smile.

I let out a hard breath. "Okay, good. So next question? Who is this pastor Renee was talking about?"

The sheriff's jaw tightened. "That's a conversation for which we need night air and warm drinks. Nine o'clock on your porch tonight?"

I nodded and then looked over to see Renee and Lucille hugging. The two women headed back toward the maze, where Nadia waited for them. Soon, those three and Officer Winslow were headed out the back door, but before they left, Renee turned and waved at me.

I swallowed back my tears and waved back. Goodness, I hoped they were going to be okay.

As soon as they were out of sight, I collapsed into my chair and gave Dad a wan smile as he walked Sawyer past me with a promise of ice cream from the shop up the street. Some very tired and Mom-oriented part of me wanted to say, "Make him eat a vegetable or fruit first," but the exhausted and still scared part of me couldn't muster the energy. He would be fine with ice cream for lunch this one day.

Santiago sat down in the chair across from me, and Mika stepped behind me and began to work the knots out of my shoulders. I held back a groan as she worked on the spot below my left shoulder blade that always ached, but I did let my head fall back and a few tears fall.

After a few moments, I looked at Santiago and said, "Thank you again."

He reached over and put his hand on my knee. "It really is my job, Paisley, but I'm glad to do it. I'm just sorry you had to go through that."

I patted his hands and let my fingers intertwine with his for just a moment before I leaned back again and sank into Mika's strong hands.

Santiago stood and said, "Time to do an interrogation. See you later?"

I lifted my head just enough to nod and smile, and then I really let Mika go to town.

6

Thirty minutes later when Dad and Sawyer returned, my body was more relaxed than it had been in weeks, and I knew I'd need to make a stop for some food of my own if I wanted to stay awake when I drove the little man for his nap. He was working through the tail end of his sugar high, and I gauged that I had approximately five minutes to get him strapped into his car seat before he went into either a meltdown or a flailing fit of play.

I scooped up my boy and tickle-carried him to the car with Dad trailing behind me carrying a small paper bag. Once I got Sawyer settled in his seat, Dad handed me the bag and said, "Quesadilla from that new Mexican place." He gestured with his head up the street a bit. "Thought you might need lunch."

I smiled and peeked in the bag. It was still warm and smelled heavenly. "Thank you, Daddy," I said, and felt my throat tighten in gratitude. I really didn't know what I would do without these people who loved me.

The drive was a gift of smoothness. Sawyer was asleep after only two plays of Blippi's "Excavator Song," and within minutes, I had lost myself completely in my latest audiobook,

Aiden Thomas's *Cemetery Boys*. Saw slept for almost two hours, and when he woke up, a slow smile slipped over his face as he met my gaze in the rearview mirror. "Ready to go home, Little Man?"

"Can we pick up sticks when we get home, Mama?" he said.

I smiled. "Of course." No child I've ever met enjoys cleaning up a yard as much as my son, and I loved it. We did need to stay on top of the branches from "God's pruning," as Dad called it, or else come mowing season, we'd need new blades before I finished half of the yard.

As soon as we pulled into the driveway, Saw was off like a shot, and before I could even get Beauregard out of the house for a little afternoon sunbathing on his kitty harness and tether, the boy had piled a ton of sticks at the edge of the yard as part of our "natural fence," a design Dad had suggested as a reasonable alternative to the elaborate stick-and-branch hedges I'd seen on Pinterest. I wanted the natural look and the bird habitat, but Dad was wise to know I didn't have hours to weave together twigs or stack branches in a checkerboard pattern.

The bonus was that Sawyer was a natural for this kind of fence-making. Pick up sticks. Toss them into a pile. He could do this for hours and sometimes did.

We spent a good bit of time building our fence before I coaxed Saw inside with the promise of baking. Next to applying mascara on my cheekbones and in my ears, baking was one of his favorite pastimes. Tonight, I decided we were going all in – calzones from homemade dough and chocolate chip cookies. We started with the pizza dough first, and Sawyer minded the mixer expertly. While the dough proofed, we mixed up the cookies and got the first batch in. Then, the moment of joy – the punching down of the dough. You'd think I'd invented candy with the delight this gave my son. Clearly, we were doing pizza dough of some sort every week now.

After the initial enthusiasm and the licking of the beater,

Sawyer's interest dwindled, and he wandered off to construct an imaginary town with his bulldozer and steamroller, and I was left with the second batch of cookies and the making of the actual calzones. I didn't mind at all – I loved to cook, and it was a delight to be able to do now that Sawyer could entertain himself for short periods at a time.

While I stuffed our dough pockets with mozzarella, pepperoni, mushrooms, and sauce, I thought about the morning and wondered again about this preacher from Mountain Green Church. I knew the building well, a plain, cinder-block structure far up the mountains in one of the most isolated and most beautiful hollows in Octonia County. Folks up that way had a reputation for being a little backward, but everyone I'd met up there was kind, if a bit more "traditional" than I was.

But this church seemed more than just run-of-the-mill politically conservative. It sounded outright misogynistic, and I didn't like the thought of a group like that being in my community. Still, until I understood what Santiago knew, I was going to reserve judgment – reserve judgment and load in some more cheese.

When Santiago arrived at nine, I was still coming out of my food stupor, but the combination of good food, that great shoulder rub from Mika, and long belly laughs with my boy had made the day end far better than it had begun. I smiled when the sheriff arrived and gave him a lingering hug fueled at first by gratitude but then by something warmer.

I blushed as I stepped back, but he just leaned over and kissed my cheek. "That was a nice welcome," he said.

The color ran deeper into my face, and I turned quickly toward the house before he could see my embarrassment. "Come in. Sawyer's out solid tonight. So much excitement for that guy today."

"For all of us, really." He stepped through the door into my butter-yellow kitchen and said, "You sure you don't mind me coming in?"

He was thoughtful to ask. "I'm sure. It's really cold out there tonight, and like I said, Sawyer is *very* asleep." When I'd crept up to check on him about an hour after he'd conked out, he was still in the same position as when I left, a puddle of drool under his cheek. It was very adorable and also very clear I needed to wash those sheets soon.

I poured hot water over peppermint tea bags in two mugs and handed one to the sheriff while I grabbed a small plate of shortbread that Lucille had dropped by this afternoon. She'd wanted to let me know that Renee and Nadia had gotten settled in at the shelter just fine. "Nadia lit up when she saw the playground and the other kids in the backyard, and when Renee found out they got their own room, she looked like she might cry."

Apparently, Scott had been worried that Renee might sneak out with Nadia some night, so he'd made them sleep in the living room on the pull-out sofa so that he could keep an eye on them. The more I learned about this guy, the more I hated him.

We settled into the love seat, and Santiago immediately put his feet up on the trunk and groaned. "Oh, it feels good to relax. It's been one of those days." He looked over at me. "For you, too."

I nodded. "I'm glad you got home to change, though. Maybe that means the day wasn't a constant go-go-go?" He was in a pair of well-worn jeans and a flannel shirt, and it was the most rustic I'd seen him. With the sparse five-o'clock shadow on his chin, he looked particularly handsome.

He smiled. "Actually, I keep these clothes at the station just in case. I went into town tonight to check on Renee and Nadia, and the folks who run the shelter prefer police officers not wear their uniforms because they draw attention from the neighbors.

The shelter is all about keeping a low profile to protect their residents." He twisted his neck and sank further into the couch.

I told him Lucille had given me the update from their arrival but asked how Renee and Nadia were doing when he saw them. "Did Renee feel safe?"

"I think so, at least from what I could tell on the security cameras. For obvious reasons, they don't let men into the house proper very often, but I could see both of them on the cameras, and they looked good, relaxed. The director said they were adjusting well, considering."

I sighed. "Maybe I could go visit sometime?"

"I think they'd like that, but maybe give them a few days to just be there without reminders of Scott." His voice was soft but clear.

"Understood," I said, and I did understand. Trauma comes with its own rules, and everybody has to heal in their own way. Renee was strong, though, and I knew she'd come through and bring Nadia right along with her. "What about Scott? Were you able to formally charge him?"

Santiago smiled. "Look at you with the police talk. Yes, Renee gave Officer Winslow a full statement once they arrived at the shelter, and we were able to arrest him on charges of domestic violence and child endangerment. If you will, we'd like you to testify to what you saw today." His expression was worried while he waited for my answer.

"Of course. Anything to help. But he didn't actually do anything but menace us before we ran." I didn't know if what I would say would mean much.

"It's just about establishing a pattern of behavior. Olivia has agreed to testify too, if the Commonwealth's Attorney needs her to do so. Her word and yours, combined with Renee's very specific statements, should be enough to convict." Santiago sounded convinced, and so I decided to be as hopeful as he was, even though everything I'd ever heard or experienced about domestic violence situations told me the chances of him being convicted were slim. Tonight, I was going to sit in hope.

I took a long sip of my tea and then said, "Tell me about Mountain Green Church."

A slim groan slipped out of Santiago's lips, and the lines around his mouth deepened. "Where to begin?" He ran his hand over his face and said, "Okay, so what we talked about before is the popular knowledge about the church. That it's a woman-hating factory disguised as a religious place."

I winced at that description but didn't doubt it. I nodded and waited for him to continue.

"But the truth is much worse than that. The pastor, Reverend Villay, is a predator. I can't tell you the number of times I've been called out to that community because he's assaulted or raped a woman from his church, only to be told, on arrival, that the call was an exaggeration, a misunderstanding." The ire behind Santiago's words was palpable.

"Someone is intimidating them into not reporting," I said matter-of-factly.

"Yes. Definitely. I just need one woman to file a formal charge, and we can investigate."

"But until then, your hands are tied." I pulled my knees up to my chest and stared into the fireplace. "I expect you've had your female officers try to talk to them."

He nodded wearily. "Several times, but they can't get into the compound."

"Wait, what?! They have a compound?" I tried to think about if I'd seen any high-walled or razor-wired groups of buildings on my drives with Sawyer out that way, but I couldn't think of anything.

"They do, but you wouldn't know it by looking. It looks like just another farm lane up there in the hollow. But if you look closely, you can see these things that look like tree stands a little ways up the lane. They're actually guard towers." He shook his head.

"They have a compound like a cult? This group is a cult? What in the world?" I wasn't sure what I was hearing.

Santiago stared at me for a minute and then shrugged. "Technically, the church would probably qualify. Most of the most devoted members live up there in the compound. And that seems like a real goal for the pastor – to bring all the members there to live. Folks who get in trouble, like Scott, usually don't stick around long because they aren't invited into the inner circle."

"What do you mean they don't stick around? Are they forced out?"

"I'm not sure. Seems like it . . . or worse." Santiago shook his head and stretched.

"So Scott is in danger, too?" I couldn't believe I even cared, but apparently I did.

"That's the thing. I think so, but he won't talk about the church at all. Clams up totally when I ask." Santiago rubbed his eyes and then stood up. "I better go. It's been a long day."

I unfolded off the couch and stood next to him. "You okay?"

He nodded as he headed for the door. "I am, and this helped. Lock the door behind me, okay?"

I smiled. "Okay." I always locked the door at night, but I knew it felt like a small way of taking care of me to remind me, so I simply smiled.

He was headed down the porch steps when he said, "I almost forgot. We're having hot cider and pumpkin donuts at the station tomorrow for the local families. A sort of meet-and-greet to build good will. Bring Sawyer by if you want. Starts at three-thirty."

"Forget Sawyer. I'd come just on my own." I waved and smiled and then stepped back inside, locked the door, and watched him drive up the lane.

Before I sat down to sew, I cranked the heat up a notch and marveled when Beauregard shifted even closer than before. One of these days that cat was going to catch himself on fire. I guess we were both chilled by what Santiago had just said: a cult in Octonia. Wow.

I picked up my hoop and untucked the silver-gray thread I'd been working with last night and started to count stitches. I was working on the boards on the barn, and they were tricky since they were all sewn in subtle shades of gray. Still, I needed to put my focus to something intense to let the events of the day and this information from Santiago sink in.

No wonder Scott was such a piece of work. I mean, I'd figured only people with some great psychological need or trauma ended up in cults. From what I'd heard about his family, he and Renee both seemed ripe for the picking by someone who wanted their allegiance in exchange for the feeling of belonging. I didn't want to feel sympathy for the man who'd scared me so badly a few hours earlier, but there it was – my big, soft heart.

I also felt frustrated on Santiago's behalf to know that people were being hurt, and hurt badly, and that he couldn't intervene. That must be the ultimate in infuriating for someone as kindhearted as the sheriff. It seemed like he had tried everything, but to no avail. I wished I could do something to help.

I worked a group of charcoal-gray stitches until I ran out of thread and let my mind focus on the in and out of the needle. The motion alone was soothing, like meditation, and if I didn't try to think too hard, the process of stitching almost always brought me clarity.

I was just coming to the end of my second length of thread for the night when it hit me. Maybe I *could* help Santiago. Maybe there was a way I could help him and Renee and even Olivia, maybe. I put down my hoop and picked up my phone.

Tomorrow is one of Mrs. Stephenson's days at the store, right? I texted Mika.

Sure is. Got something in mind?

Feel like infiltrating a cult?

Not exactly your normal Thursday activity, but tell me more. Breakfast at the coffee shop? Seven-thirty?

See you there.

My next call was to my stepmother, and she was delighted to hear Sawyer would come by about nine. "We'll bake mini cheesecakes. I just found a new recipe." I could hear the joy in her voice. I promised her I'd be back by eleven-thirty to drive him for his nap, and she said that would be perfect because she had ballet class in town at twelve-fifteen. I smiled and hung up. Only my seventy-two-year-old stepmother would take ballet.

SAWYER WAS NOT an easy child to get moving in the morning. He didn't like to get dressed. He didn't like to eat. He didn't like to go outside early. Mostly, he liked to play with his toy trucks, drink chocolate milk, and snuggle Beauregard. I didn't care most mornings. Let the boy enjoy lazy mornings while he could. Soon enough, school and then work would replace those hours of leisurely waking up.

That next morning, though, I needed to move him along. Fortunately, the promise of time with Auntie Mickie, a chocolate croissant, and then a visit to Boppy and Baba's got him going, and when he wouldn't change out of his pj's, I didn't even try. I just stuffed his clothes for the day into his backpack and loaded him up. With his bed head and his "Rumbling Off to Sleep" dump truck pajamas, he was mighty cute. It kind of felt fun for Mika (and the town) to see him this way, and he loved it. "I'm going to get coffee in my pj's, Mama," he kept telling me in the rearview mirror.

"You are, Love Bug. What a treat."

"I like this treat," he said before begging another round of "The Party Freeze Dance Song."

After a good old dance- and sing-along on the ride, Sawyer and I were both in a giddy mood as we parked, settled Beau on his fleece blanket in Saw's car seat, and headed quickly to the coffee shop. Sawyer had only allowed me to drape his coat over his shoulders, and his teddy bear slippers were not really built for thirty-degree days. But he laughed the whole way. "It's an adventure, Mama."

"Sawyer Boy, what are you wearing?" Mika squealed as we came in. "You look so cozy."

"I is cozy, Auntie Mickie." His greeting duties done, he turned to me and said, "Chocolate crayon please."

I laughed. "One chocolate croissant coming up. Get you anything?" I asked Mika, who was tickling Saw until he squealed.

"I'll take a chocolate crayon, too," she said, "but here, use this." She stopped the tickle attack long enough to fish a gift card out of her pocket. "A store patron left it for me, said I needed to treat myself sometimes, so I'm treating all of us."

I looked at the card and smiled because I recognized that gift card. Lucille and Dad kept a supply of them on her desk to give away anonymously whenever they could. But Mika didn't need to know that. "Great! Thanks," I said.

I got our three chocolate "crayons," one apple juice, and two vanilla lattes and sat down at the table. Mika had already gotten out her phone, which was preloaded with kids' videos, and Sawyer barely looked up when I slid the definitely-not-heated croissant in front of him. Sawyer would try any food at long as it was room temperature.

"So what's this with the cult?" Mika glanced at Sawyer and then back at me. I shook my head. He didn't know that word, so we could talk about it freely.

"The sheriff was telling me that's what Mountain Green is.

Did you know that?" I explained about the compound and the guard towers, and then I told her about the reports of assaults happening to women there. I didn't expound on that, given the young ears nearby, but I didn't need to. Mika's face was grim.

"I've heard about some women from up in the Hollow being"—she paused and looked at Sawyer—"assaulted and then refusing to press charges, but I didn't realize they were connected."

"Do you know any of the women personally?"

Mika shook her head. "No. Well, one woman who I heard had been, um, assaulted comes into the shop from time to time, but she never talks much and always pays cash. I only know it's her because Mrs. Stephenson told me her name once. Then, when I heard some other customers talking about 'that poor girl Marge,' I made the connection."

I paused and thought for a minute. "Does Mrs. Stephenson live up that way near the church?"

"Yep. Third, maybe fourth generation up there. She's very proud of her heritage," Mika said with a smile.

"A true Octonian then," I chuckled. "Do you think she could tell you any more about the church?"

"We're talking about that gray block church on the corner, right, just below that new winery?"

I nodded.

"I expect so, then, she just lives up the road a little. Want me to ask her when I stop in later?"

"Yeah, but just in general. I don't want her to know it has anything to do with Rocket's, er, demise," I said.

Sawyer looked up at me briefly like he knew we were talking around him, but soon Diana and Roma were in a pool and he was lost in the screen again.

"Got it. Now, what's the plan for this morning?"

I'd woken up in the middle of the night with anxiety tight in my chest, and so instead of tossing and turning, I'd gotten up to think. My plan wasn't sophisticated, but I hoped it might work since, as two single, middle-aged women, we would probably look weak and desperate to the men of Mountain Green. We'd use the hateful stereotype to our advantage.

"We drive up and ask for a tour. Tell them we've heard that their community protects women and wanted to see for ourselves." I suddenly felt nervous as I waited to see what Mika thought.

She tilted her head and looked out the window behind me for a moment and said, "I think that could work, but we do need to address why we wouldn't just go to church services first, right? I mean, wouldn't that seem like the easier way?"

I grinned. "I thought of that, too, but I think we can say that we were worried about word getting out if we went somewhere so public, that my dad might object, and so we wanted to see if we were serious enough to put ourselves in 'danger' first."

Mika laughed.

"What's so funny?" I snapped.

"Oh, sorry. Nothing. That sounds possible. I was just laughing because the idea of your dad thinking he could 'object' to anything in your life is laughable."

I smiled. My dad had always respected my right to make my own decisions, even when he didn't understand them, and even if he hadn't trusted me to make my own choices, he knew better than to intervene once I was a grown woman. Dad wasn't exactly a feminist, but he had loved several of them and was wise enough not to try and tell us what to do.

Sawyer had finished his "crayon" and had as much chocolate on his face as in it and had moved onto videos of toy marketers running monster trucks through sand piles, so Mika and I polished up our strategy. Last night, I'd told her to dress plainly and modestly, and she'd come in baggy jeans and a loose black sweater that looked like one she might have owned since junior high and worn with leggings. I'd managed to drag a long blue skirt out of the back of my closet and had put on a loose white blouse and a navy cardigan. I felt like my fourth-grade teacher, Ms. Mackey, in this get-up, but I figured the more schoolmarmish we looked, the better.

Fully caffeinated and sugared-up, we climbed into my car for the ride to Dad and Lucille's. Once we arrived, Mika took on the daunting task of getting Sawyer dressed, and from the laughter issuing from the back seat as I removed Beauregard from his heated seat so that he could lay on the blanketed love seat in Dad's living room, I think they were both enjoying themselves. The four of us trundled into the house with smiles on our faces.

Lucille was all set for baking cheesecake. She'd even gotten Little Man a new stool that put his hands at just the right height to "help." Fortunately, Lucille was a seasoned grandmother and baker, and she'd already prepped most things, leaving just the simple act of mixing for Sawyer, who soon came in squealing with delight as Mika chanted, "I'm gonna catch you. Here I come. I'm gonna catch you. You better run."

Their game continued just long enough for Sawyer to glimpse the baking supplies, and then he was on that stool saying, "I ready to help."

Lucille winked at me, and Mika and I went back into Dad's workshop to say hello. He was in the process of building a platform bird feeder for the farmhouse, and it looked amazing. Dad was a master at pulling together beautiful things from scraps, and this was no exception with its edges made from various colors of used quarter-round and a repurposed stairwell newel post.

Dad and I made a great team because whatever I salvaged that turned out to not be worth much, Dad would turn into something. This newel post I'd pulled out of an old house in the next town a few weeks back, but it was cracked at the base and would have been too short to meet building codes if we chopped it down to make it sturdy. So, voilà, it was now going to be my bird feeder.

"Looks great, Mr. S.," Mika said. "Could I trouble you to make me one of these?"

"Already got it started," Dad said and pointed to a pile of scrap wood that I knew he could already envision as a bird-feeder. To me, it looked like the start of a good bonfire. "Have it for you next week."

Mika beamed. "Thank you. I just saw my first flicker the other day, and I want to draw them closer."

"Same here," I said, "and I'm hoping it will give Beauregard something to do besides sleep. By the way, he's in your spot on the couch." It never failed that when Beau came to visit, he took Dad's seat. It was like the law for my cat – find the person who most dislikes you and take up their space.

Dad grimaced and went back to sanding.

"We're off to visit Mountain Green Church," Mika said as she turned to go, and I winced.

"You're going where?" Dad said, acting as if he hadn't heard when I knew perfectly well, from the expression on his face, that he heard what she said loud and clear.

Mika turned back around slowly. "Mountain Green Church?" Her statement had turned into a question.

Dad glanced at me and then went back to the bird feeder. "Why would you want to go messing around up there?"

I took a deep breath. The less interested Dad looked, the more interested he was. "Curiosity," I said, careful to tell the truth but not reveal too much.

"You know that killed the cat, right?" Dad smiled just a bit, pleased with his own cleverness. But then his face went dark again. "You be careful."

I nodded. Dad didn't lecture or give advice very often, but when he did, I listened. By which I mean I heard what he said but intended to do whatever I was planning anyway, just with his advice in mind. “We will, Daddy,” I said and patted his hand.

“Let’s go,” I hissed to Mika.

She hustled after me as I threw a goodbye and I love you to Sawyer. He didn’t even respond.

When we got outside, Mika said, “I slipped up, huh?”

“You couldn’t know, but Dad has very strong opinions about certain groups of people in Octonia, including the folks who live up in that Hollow. I don’t know what he knows about the church in specific, but his reaction told me he doesn’t like the idea of us being up there.”

“That makes me more nervous,” Mika said as she slid into the passenger’s seat after peeling off Beau’s fur-covered blanket.

“Me, too,” I said quietly.

7

The sun was out and the winter day was crisp, so the ride up and over into the Hollow was gorgeous. The beeches still had their leaves, and beneath the towering oaks and poplars, they danced in the slight breeze. People always talked about the beauty of spring, but I thought winter was the forgotten stunner.

The Hollow was a narrow passage up into the heart of the Blue Ridge Mountains. Many of the residents there had originally lived further up the mountainside but had been forced out when Roosevelt commissioned the Shenandoah National Park. People were still pretty bitter about the way their land had been taken from them, and honestly, I couldn't blame them. It was a nasty little bit of Virginia history.

Maybe that's where the reputation about the Hollow being dangerous and backwards had come from, from that anger that still rankled in the folds of the hills. Or maybe it came from the poverty that sat like a fog over the houses where people couldn't afford to haul away old car bodies or appliances. Or maybe it was some part prejudice and some part truth. I wasn't sure, but I'd grown up knowing that the Hollow wasn't a place I should really go by myself.

Mika's presence helped, of course, but I was still nervous as all get-out, especially after Dad's warning. But I tried to focus on the beautiful day and the scenery. We stopped first at the church and pretended to be looking for a particular name on the tombstones there so that we could look around. The building was simple, with no stained glass windows or even much landscaping. From what I could tell without appearing too suspicious and looking in the windows, the structure included a small sanctuary and some sort of recreational space at the back, maybe a fellowship hall and a Sunday School classroom or two.

When we walked around the back, we saw tasteful, clean, and big outdoor bathrooms, one for men and one for women. The fact that the church didn't have running water wasn't all that rare up here, actually. Plumbing was expensive, and sometimes digging a well was tricky on the mountainside. But I was still a bit surprised to see that a church hadn't gone to the trouble of installing indoor bathrooms.

The names on the tombstones were ones I recognized from this part of Octonia. Lots of Shifletts – but with only one *F*, which, despite their shared heritage way back, told me that this part of the family was quite distinct from Santiago's line. Morris, Cox, Snow, Malone, Chapman – all names that had graced public offices and roads around the county for as long as I could remember. Some of the stones looked to be from the nineteenth century. The decoration and deterioration gave them away as from another time.

When the third car coming down the mountain slowed to stare at us, we decided we'd best be on our way. It was only when I started further up into the Hollow that I told Mika I didn't exactly know where we were going.

She whipped her face in my direction and stared at me

before shaking her head and smiling. "Okay, so what are we looking for, then?

I told her about the country lane and the guard towers that looked like tree stands for hunters. "From what Santiago said, there are two, which should stand out." Hunters used tree stands all the time up here because they gave them a clear view up and over the undergrowth at deer or turkeys or the occasional bear. But they were usually spread out for safety and also to eliminate competition. Two on opposite sides of a lane should be distinctive, and I was hoping that with the leaves off the trees we'd see them easily.

We drove all the way up to the top of the Hollow, where the old CCC fire road became almost impassable as it crossed into the National Park, but we hadn't yet seen the right lane. I hadn't felt it wise to slow down too much at each possible entrance, and so we might have missed it. I figured we had one more shot to try and find it as we headed back the way we came, and if we couldn't find it, we'd disguise our trip by turning at the church and going up to the winery. They weren't open yet, but we could act like we didn't know that, should anyone ask. I was really hoping they wouldn't ask.

Fortunately, just as we were almost back to the church and our intended turn, Mika shouted and pointed across me to the north side of the road. "I think that's it. See?"

I slowed just a bit after being sure no one was behind me, and then I saw them: two weathered stands nestled into the arms of two big oaks trees. "I do."

I put on my blinker, apparently to signal the deer, since there wasn't another car in sight, and pulled in and tried to decide how to proceed. I was of two minds at that moment. Did I move through quickly on the well-maintained road, acting as if it was as normal as day that I'd turned in? Or did I go slowly and let them know I knew they were there? I wasn't sure which would be help sell our story more effectively.

I opted, after just a moment, to plow right ahead. I'd been driving gravel roads my whole life, and if there were people here who recognized my car, and surely there were, it might look suspicious if I crept along. After all, I was supposed to be curious, not suspicious. I zoomed right ahead and marveled at the perfect crowning and ditching that kept the water from washing the road out, even as we began to climb up the mountainside again.

The tree stands were about a quarter mile up the lane just at the tree line, and even when we got to them, I could have easily missed them if a bright orange flag hadn't waved from behind one and caused me to slow down enough that I didn't hit the large man who stepped into the middle of the road just beyond the flag. I didn't recognize him personally, but he looked a lot like many older men from around here: white, bearded, and a little pissed off. He was wearing camo coveralls, and I could only hope he was really guarding and not hunting. A hunter in this secluded spot would have worked hard for his game, and if he was hunting, the deer musk he might have used to cover his own body's scent would be really unpleasant as soon as I opened my window.

He held his hand up, palm out toward the car, and I slowed to a stop. Out of the corner of my eye, I saw Mika check her phone in her lap and then shake her head. No signal. My heart rate picked up.

The man stepped up to my window and smiled. "What can I do you ladies for?"

The syntax of his sentence was normally a charming part of our mountain dialect, but given the situation and the slight leer to this man's smile, it just struck me as sinister in that moment.

"We were told by a woman I met at my shop that this might be a place we could come, um, to be safe." Mika sounded scared, but just in the right way, not scared of *here* but scared in general.

The man stood back and said, "Were you now? Well, we'll have to thank Marge for sending us two beauties, won't we, Lyle?" He looked through the car windows to the man who was now by Mika's window.

All the moisture in my mouth disappeared. He knew about Marge. I had to take a deep breath and hope my smile looked forced and timid because I was terrified, in all the ways.

Fortunately, Mika was quick on her feet. "She's so humble that I'm sure she won't take any credit." Mika looked down at the floor as if she, too, were meek and mild. "I hope we didn't do anything wrong coming up." She glanced up at the man by her window and then quickly back at the floor. My best friend was brazen and brash and a little bit crass, so I was surprised at how well she could pull off the browbeaten maiden look.

But then, most of the women I knew had needed that look from time to time just to avoid the abuse that could rain down on any female who spoke her mind. I took a deep breath and channeled the version of myself that let a boss bully me for years because he didn't like that I didn't wear heels to work every day.

"Do you mind if we go up? Do we need an escort?" I made my voice a little thin and wavery and refused to acknowledge the queasiness this acting job made me feel.

The man by my window studied my face another moment, but I kept my eyes down on my hands in my lap until he spoke. "I suppose a quick drive through would be fine, young ladies." He cackled briefly at his own insult. "Just don't get out of the car until one of us can take you into any of the buildings, okay?"

"Sure," Mika said eagerly. "Thank you."

"Yes, thank you," I repeated and smiled up at the man by my window without meeting his eyes.

"See you up there in a minute," he said and then patted the hood of my car like it was a horse's rear. I put the car in drive and moved ahead slowly, keeping an eye on my rearview mirror. The Santa man pulled a walkie-talkie out of his pocket and made a call, and the other guy climbed back up into his stand.

Mika leaned over and whispered, "He looks like a malevolent Santa Claus."

I stifled a nervous giggle and nodded.

A few moments later, we met a Jeep coming down the hill. I pulled off as far as I could, but I needn't have bothered. The Jeep just wheeled up the bank by the side of the road and hung at a forty-five-degree angle while we passed.

I kept my eyes straight ahead, but I saw Mika sneak a quick look over before turning back to the road. Once we were by, she said, "White dude. About forty-five. Clean-shaven. Handsome, kind of, but in that way some serial killers are handsome."

"Dexter Syndrome," we said in unison and laughed. The sound broke the tension in the car just a little. Both of us had tried to watch the TV series *Dexter* a few years back, but we'd had to stop – separately, but at about the same point in the show – because we found him too attractive and couldn't get out of our own heads about thinking a serial killer was dreamy. Now, whenever a scary guy is also hot, we whip out our shorthand term, "Dexter Syndrome."

I didn't know how long this drive was, but I knew Mika and I had to make a plan for what we were going to do up there. "So we're not going in any buildings, right?" I said.

"Are you kidding? I am not getting trapped in some cult building if they decide to end it all or if the FBI comes raiding. I will not die in the Octonia version of Ruby Ridge," Mika said.

"Agreed. So we drive through. If they ask us to stop, we try to stay in the car, but if we must, we can walk around outside but not go inside. Sound good?"

"I like it," Mika said, "but how do we keep from being given the whole tour? I mean, if we're really interested, wouldn't we want to see everything?"

She had a point, and I had no idea. I thought briefly of saying I had an allergy to chemicals in perfumes and cleaning products and hoping that might keep us outside. Then, I considered telling them that we didn't like to be in enclosed spaces with men and let them infer what they would, but fortunately, my cell phone chirped just as we came into a clearing at the top of a ridgeline. I paused just at the edge of the trees and read the message from Santiago.

You doing okay today?

Yep. *But do me a favor? Call me in fifteen minutes. Keep calling until I answer. I'll explain later if you promise not to be mad.*

**groan* Okay . . . but no promises.*

Thanks.

I LOOKED at Mika and nodded. "We have our out."

She sighed and turned to look at the windshield again. "We're going in."

"We're going in," I said as I let the car roll out into the sunshine. The landscape was breathtaking with mountains climbing up beyond the clearing and tall, thick trees running all along the forest's edge. I doubt this was virgin woods up here – too much lumber had come out of these mountains for there to be much left of the forests the Monacan Indians knew, but these trees were old, a couple hundred years old at least. Dad would have loved it.

But the buildings in this field were a little creepy. It took me a minute to figure out why they gave me the willies, but then I pictured Ben Linus from *Lost* standing by one of the little cabins to my right. It looked remarkably like the Dharma Initiative Compound, what with the little ranch-style cabins and the central building, which was meant, I thought, to look like a lodge but really looked more like a wood-clad high school from the 1940s.

People were walking on mulched paths between the buildings, and everyone looked like they were content, at least as far as I could tell from a distance. The road appeared to continue on through the buildings, and on the pretext of looking like we really did want to see everything, I kept driving. The further in we went, though, the more looks we got, and soon, everyone on the walkways had stopped and was staring. Clearly, they didn't get many visitors.

I was about to pull into a small parking area and turn around when Santa Man and another very thin man with skin the color of the paste that Sawyer had tried to eat the previous weekend walked toward us at a brisk pace. I decided I was at least going to point the car in the get-away direction, so I quickly turned around in the grass by the side of the road and began heading back out the way we came, certain we had seen anything we were "allowed" to see and not wanting to take the risk of seeing something we really shouldn't.

But soon, the men had reached the car, and Santa Man stepped into the road and, again, put up his hand for us to stop. He was very trusting of my driving ability, very confident of his own power, or very stupid. Clearly, he had no worries that I would gun it and run right over him. I wouldn't, but still, he didn't know that. So I was going with stupid, if only because it made me feel better.

I let the car come to a stop and rolled down my window. "Hi, again," I said brightly and then immediately realized I sounded self-possessed and strong and lowered my eyes to say, "Thank you for letting us come through. It's beautiful here."

The second man stepped forward, and I was instantly reminded of a skeleton. He was so thin that I could see his cheekbones more clearly than I could see Christian Bale's ribs in that movie where he lost something like sixty pounds for a role. He looked profoundly unwell, and at first, I thought the impression came just from the pallor of his skin and his thinness. But then I also realized that he was grinning like a mad scientist. I was pretty sure I could see his molars from the way his mouth was peeled back into what I knew must have been meant to be a welcoming expression. Instead, he looked like a character from a Tim Burton film.

"Hello there," the man said without extending his hand. "I'm Reverend Villay. Nicholas here tells me that you women are interested in our community. I'd love to give you the full tour, show you around."

I looked over at Mika and tried to act like I was actually seeing what she'd say. She nodded and opened the door on her side of the car to step out. Before she did, I squeezed her fingers and felt her phone in her hand. Good, we were both prepared.

I stepped out, carefully sliding my own phone into the deep pocket of my skirt as I stood up. "Thank you, Reverend Villay. We don't want to trouble you, though. I know you must have important work for your congregation."

The pastor nodded his head in a gesture I'd seen profoundly arrogant people use again and again to feign humility. It seemed to say, "Yes, I do have great work to do, but I will allow you to bask in my greatness for a bit." I swallowed to keep from grimacing.

"Please, it would be my pleasure. Nicholas here tells me that Marge suggested you come."

I took a deep breath. The last thing we wanted to do was get Marge in trouble, especially with this guy.

"Not exactly," Mika said as she tucked a lock of hair behind her ear. "I just overheard her talking about her friends here, about how they supported her, about how the men here really know how to take care of a woman."

I stepped toward her and took her hand as she pretended to wipe away a tear. "My friend has had a hard couple of years with her ex," I said, and hoped these two dudes were bright enough to pick up on the implication without me having to spell out Mika's fake backstory of abuse. I really didn't want to risk giving too many details that we'd need to keep track of. "She's . . ." I looked over at Mika, who smiled. "We're looking for a place we can call home, where we can contribute without the dangerous influences of society."

Something in that spiel hit the reverend right because his grin turned from a tortured pull on his mouth to something more real but no less creepy. "Well, women, you've come to the right place then."

Normally, when people refer to those of us who identify as female with the word "women," I'm grateful because the alternatives are often "girls" or "ladies," both terms that reek with condescension. But this man using the word "women" set my teeth on edge. It felt like he was talking about mealworms or something, like we were disgusting but useful. I shuddered as the men turned to lead the way toward the large building.

It felt like it had been close to fifteen minutes, and I knew Santiago wouldn't miss the time. I just hoped the call would come before we got inside. I didn't know how long Mika and I could keep up this act, and I didn't want to be caught inside if we slipped up. Too hard to get away.

Reverend Villay was telling us about how everyone in the community also attended the church at the bottom of the lane. "I heard you stopped by and visited our cemetery. Since you are a historian, Ms. Sutton, I expect you appreciated the age of some of the graves."

I tried not to look shocked that he not only knew we'd been at the church but also who I was and what I did, but since I couldn't form words, I wasn't very smooth. "Um, yeah," I grunted.

"Don't be alarmed. We have simple security cameras at the church to discourage vandalism, and we like to know who visits us so we can tailor our tour to their needs. Ms. Sutton, if you share your father's love of trees, I expect you'll want to visit our beautiful white oak here in the center of the green. We estimate it is over three hundred years old. We use it as the center of our space to remind us that our roots – both in this place and in our faith – are deep." He gestured with a soft sweep of his hand toward a massive oak in the center of the field before us.

It was gorgeous, with wide branches that spun and bent toward the light. It reminded me of the great oak down by the airport, a tree I loved to pass when I came up from Charlottesville that way. But this one was bigger, and its canopy was even more massive. I wanted to go sit under her.

Reverend Villay's voice snapped me out of her spell like a splash of ice water in the face. "Mika Andrews, your store is the favorite of many of the women here. Just last week, one of our members bought yarn to make a blanket for the new addition who was born here yesterday. You may remember? I think she bought eight skeins of pink bamboo yarn." He smiled like it was completely normal for a pastor to know how many skeins of what color and type of yarn a member of his church had bought.

Mika didn't miss a beat, though. "I do remember. I hope the baby and mother are healthy." She smiled innocently, but I knew there was a larger query behind that simple question.

"Completely. Healthy eight-pound three-ounce girl. Mama was up and about the next day helping us dig leeks for our evening meal." He pointed toward the building ahead of us. "Inside here, well, let me just show you." He stepped forward to open the door, and I shuddered. Short of bolting to the car – and I'd already done that one time too many this week – I didn't see how we could get out of going in.

But just then, my phone rang in my pocket. I fumbled with the awkward fabric of the skirt for a moment and gave what I hoped looked like a sincerely sorry expression as I answered, "Hello?"

"Paisley, are you okay?" Santiago's voice was worried. "You sound funny."

"Oh, Sheriff, what can I do for you?" I saw Santa Man and Reverend Villay stiffen for just a moment as I spoke. "Did you need something else from me about that incident yesterday?"

If Mountain Green Church was as connected as I thought they were, they would know all about Scott Morris's arrest. I was hoping this would make a good cover for the call and for why we had to leave.

"You're with someone?" Santiago said. "You need me to call you away?"

I nodded. "Yes, sir, that's right."

"Okay, then, I need you at the station immediately to clarify some details of the events in the park." His voice had taken on a firm edge.

"Yes, Sheriff. I'll be right there. We're just up in the Hollow, but I'll come right away." I made my voice shake just a little for effect. It may have been overacting, but I really wanted to sell the downtrodden woman bit.

I hung up the phone and turned to Reverend Villay and Santa Man. "I'm sorry. Really sorry," I said without meeting their eyes. "The sheriff is making me come to the station because of something that happened yesterday."

Mika stepped over and hugged me. "Not that again. Hasn't that man put you through enough?"

I grabbed a balled up receipt that was in my other skirt pocket and pretended to wipe my eyes with it. "I just want to help that poor man who is being persecuted." I was laying it on thick now.

"You mean Scott Morris?" Santa Man asked as he stepped toward me. "What does the sheriff want to do to him now? He already arrested him."

I sniffed. "I don't know. That man was just trying to protect his sister, and she made me take her to the police. I didn't really know what was going on . . ."

Mika put her arm through mine. "You did what you had to do to protect you and your son, Paisley. Come on. I'll go with you and be a witness if that sheriff tries to browbeat you into anything that isn't true."

Reverend Villay's face was flat, unaffected, but I could see his fingers twitching against the leg of his perfectly pressed pants. "Well, I'm sorry the tour has been cut short, especially under these circumstances. But do come to church some Sunday. Meet some people."

I looked at Mika who smiled and said, "We'd like that. What time is the service?"

"Eleven a.m.," Santa man said, "like worship should be."

Outside, I smiled. Inside, I rolled my eyes. These people really were back in the dark ages if they thought the "right" time for worship was eleven a.m. Goodness.

We made our way quickly back to the car with the two men – and most everyone else in the community – watching us. Mika, playing the role of good friend, helped me to the passenger side of the car and then got into the driver's seat. Obviously, I was too upset about what was about to happen to drive.

The men waved as we moved down the lane, and Mika kept her speed steady and even until we were out on the Hollow Road and out of sight of the guard stands. Then, she gunned it and said, "You do realize that Santa's name is Nicholas, right?"

8

On the not-so-off chance that Reverend Villay had us tailed, we did, indeed, go straight to the police station, and when I saw a pickup truck crawl by the parking lot as we got out and pretended to need to lean on each other for moral support rather than because we were still laughing hysterically over the fact that Santa Man was actually named Nicholas, I knew we'd made a good choice.

Inside, the deputy at the front desk told us that Santiago was waiting and sent us down the hall with a smirk as we continued to break out in bursts of laughter and wipe the tears from our eyes. My belly ached in the best way, and the laughing was a much-needed tension reliever.

But unfortunately, as soon as I saw Santiago's face, all that tension came rushing right back. His lips were thin, and the look he gave me when we walked in sucked the last bit of laughter out of my chest.

"What were you thinking?" he asked in a voice that was more piercing because of its quietness.

I stared at him for a moment and then I collapsed into a chair. "I'm sorry," I said. "It's just that you said you couldn't get up there, and all I could think about was Renee, and all those other women . . . and all my friends who have never gotten justice . . ." I knew I was rambling, and I could feel the tears threatening to tumble after all the words, but I couldn't stop myself. I looked over at Mika, and she looked about to cry, too. My words finally stumbled to a halt, and I sat and waited for the lecture.

Instead, Santiago sat down, dropped his head, and said, "I'm sorry. As soon as you said you were in the Hollow, I knew what you were doing, and I was terrified, Paisley. But I understand why you did what you did. And it worked." He looked up at me then. "At least I hope it worked."

Mika and I looked at each other, and then we both began to nod with vigor. "It did work," she said. "We got in, and we got the offer of a tour."

"Plus an invitation to church on Sunday." I felt a little smug just saying it. "They know all about Scott, too, and they didn't look any too happy that he'd been arrested. We actually used him to play off your call, so if anyone asks, you demanded we come in, okay?"

A smile slowly spread across the sheriff's mouth. "Got it. Now, tell me everything you saw, and let's make a plan for Sunday."

I stared at him for a moment before I could speak. "You want us to go?"

"Want and need are two different things. But first, give me the scoop." He pulled his notepad close and jotted down notes about everything we said, from the tree stands at the entrance to the *Lost*-like houses and the big building that looked like a horrible hospital for people with mental illnesses.

Mika included another detail that I hadn't thought to put into words. "And all the women were in skirts and had their hair up. They looked sort of Mennonite, but less stylish."

I nodded. "She's right. Mennonite women are fastidious

about their appearance, and they make their cape dresses out of beautiful fabrics. These women looked like they bought their clothes from the dollar rack at the Goodwill without trying them on."

Santiago looked up briefly. "Did you see any bruises on any of the women? Notice any limps? Anything physical?"

I scanned my memory, hoping something would snag, but ultimately had to shake my head. "No, nothing like that. If they have physical injuries, they are hiding them well." When Santiago's shoulders drooped, I said, "Would that have helped?"

"Maybe. It would have, at least, been something further to take to a judge for a search warrant." He sighed and went back to his notes. "Did you see any guns?"

"Just the ones at the entrance," Mika said, "but I wouldn't be surprised if they don't have armed people everywhere. It just felt like that kind of place, you know."

I nodded. "Especially since they followed us here."

Mika jumped up. "What?! They followed us here? I didn't see anyone."

"I just noticed the truck when we got out of the car. 1980s-ish pickup, brown and tan. Virginia plates. I think they started with a P8, or something like that." I had tried to see as much detail as I could before the truck went around the corner.

"I didn't even notice," Mika said as she slumped back into the wooden chair in front of Santiago's desk. "Glad you were paying attention."

"Me, too," the sheriff said as he stood up. "Be right back."

I reached over and took Mika's hand. She looked again like she might cry. "You okay?"

She nodded and said, "I think I'm just now realizing how scared I was. Those people are super-duper creepy."

I sighed. "They are . . . I had to keep imagining we were Velma and Daphne from *Scooby Doo* just to keep myself from freaking out."

That brought out a smile on Mika's face. "Is Santiago Fred then? And who is Shaggy?"

I giggled. "Sawyer. I'm teaching him to say 'Zoinks' tonight." I started laughing again, and I could feel the workout my abs were getting. I'd take the exercise when I could get it.

Mika was smiling, too, and said, "So that makes Beauregard Scooby? He will *not* like that."

I cackled and said, "He doesn't like anything. We'll get him the blue collar, and he'll be fine. He is kind of a fashion maven, that cat."

When Santiago returned, we were imagining who we'd find hiding under Santa Man's mask at the end of our episode. Mika had just suggested an elf, and I was literally doubled over in hysterics.

"Okay, you two. You need some coffee, a brisk walk, and naps. You're out of control." Santiago's voice was authoritative, but I could still hear his smile and I forced myself to stand up and head for the door.

"Maybe we can talk about the plan for Sunday later today. I think you're right that we need a little break," I managed to say before I started laughing again.

"Mika's shop at three. We can use our secret clubhouse," he said and sent us into fits of laughter again.

"Totally, Fred," Mika laughed as we walked out the door.

MIKA and I were both pretty broke, so we swung by to get Sawyer and headed back to my house for some good old PB&J and potato chips. Sawyer detested the childhood classic, so he had vegetable-infused chicken nuggets and boxed mac and cheese. But I made Mika and me sandwiches with extra-crunchy peanut butter and the great freezer jam Lucille had made this summer. Add in salt-and-vinegar chips and some sweet tea, and it was a delightful meal in the sunshine of the farmhouse kitchen.

Soon, Sawyer was out the door and climbing up the garden fence so he could straddle the doghouse Dad and he had built last week. He had his toolbox and was putting on some finishing touches, it seemed. Mika and I strolled through the yard and talked about the morning in lots of detail.

In the end, we came to the conclusion that the Mountain Green Compound was outright creepy, that the women looked like they could have walked right out of *The Handmaid's Tale*, even without the red dresses and headpieces, and that Reverend Villay was easily the creepiest man we'd ever met. We also agreed that at times in our lives when things had been really hard, the kind of life that place promised, where every decision was made for you and your position in the daily happenings was very clear, would have been quite tempting.

"I'm so glad I have a good sense of myself now," I said. "But twenty-seven-year-old Paisley? She could have ended up there. No doubt."

Mika sighed. "Thirty-year-old Mika could have, too. That's the thing, right? Even Scott is a sort of victim here. Reverend Villay is preying on people who are vulnerable."

I nodded. "Which makes me wonder if Rocket got in his way? I mean, what if he confronted Reverend Villay about Scott? It sounds like they were friends, at least at some point."

Mika bent down and added another stick to the pile she'd been gathering as we walked. "Might be worth asking Renee about that."

"I think I'll do just that," I said before I was distracted by the fact that my toddler was walking the garden fence like it was a balance beam. I had to give it to him, he could be an Olympian with that technique.

An hour later, we were in Mika's shop, where Mrs. Stephenson had graciously offered to keep Sawyer busy while we talked to the sheriff. Mika had called her to let her know we were coming in and to ask her to "tighten up security" around the new conversation nook. When we arrived, the two wing-back chairs and a lovely club chair printed in a vibrant paisley pattern were surrounded by a floor-to-ceiling ensemble of bins full of yarn that were arranged according to rainbow order. The whole setup was absolutely gorgeous, and it even more completely screened the conversation area from the front window.

"Wow, Mrs. S.," Mika said, "you went all out. Where's this new chair from?"

"I had Mr. S. bring it down. It was just sitting in the corner of our basement, and I thought you'd need three seats. Keep it as long as you like." She smiled and then followed after Sawyer at the perfect distance to prevent him from injuring himself but also to allow him the freedom to explore. She was a natural.

"She's amazing. I know she's been coming here a long time to knit, but beyond that, I know nothing. She's not from here, is she?"

Mika laughed. "Well, by most standards, yes she is. She's lived here for fifty years. But in Octonia standards, no, she wasn't born here."

I grimaced. "Eek, sorry." I hated when people pulled out the "locals are the only ones who know" card, and I'd just done it.

"No biggie. She'd laugh. She actually ran her own business as an accountant for a lot of years while she was raising her kids. Now that she's retired, she wanted to be more 'out and about,' she said. I guess working from home for all that time could wear on you, but most days, it sounds pretty great to me."

I nodded. "I do love it, but I'm only a few years in. Ask me in a decade if I still appreciate being able to stay in pj's until ten." I smiled. "An accountant, huh? I wouldn't have figured."

Mika nodded. "A good one, too. She came highly recommended when I opened the shop. She had just retired, but she took me on as a client anyway because she wanted to support another businesswoman."

Mrs. Stephenson was helping Sawyer get inside the huge wine barrel that Mika had recently acquired to store her bargain yarn in. My son was cackling with glee, and I loved it.

"And now she works here, and you're supporting her in a new way as a working woman. I love it," I said.

Just then, Santiago came in, and Mika and I quickly ducked into the conversation corner so that if someone was watching from outside, it wouldn't be possible to see us talking together. The sheriff had thought to put on plain clothes and was wearing a ball cap. I would have recognized him from a thousand paces or more, but I'm not sure most people would have, not with the huge puffy jacket he was wearing.

"Borrow that from one of the high schoolers?" I teased as he sat down next to me.

"Very funny. I wanted to look a bit different, for obvious reasons. It was left in the Board of Supervisors' meeting room a few months ago, and since it's just been sitting in Lost and Found, I liberated it." Santiago tugged the giant jacket off and immediately looked more comfortable.

"It suits you," Mika said with a grin. "Planning a TikTok party later?"

"Look, you," he said and shot her a fake grimace. "Okay, so let's talk about what you two are going to do about the fact that you are now being vetted by Mountain Green Church."

Mika and I turned to each other and then, as if choreographed, faced Santiago again. "What do you mean?" I said.

"There are two church members on the street right now, watching the store. I expect they've had their eyes on you since you made your visit earlier today." He looked at me sternly.

I thought of Sawyer playing in the yard and Mika and I just walking around. My hands went numb with fear. "They were at my house?"

Santiago nodded. "I expect so, if that's where you were before you came back here, and this time, we can't have an officer with you, or it will tip them off. Unless you would rather not go through with this at all. If that's the case, I totally understand." He met my eyes and nodded. "Totally understand."

A few weeks earlier, I'd inadvertently gotten myself into a police situation (and the start of a relationship with the sheriff) where I needed twenty-four-hour police protection. And here I was again, in danger, but this time, I'd made the choice to get into it. A basketball-sized knot of worry settled into my stomach.

I looked at Mika, and despite the panic in her eyes, she said, "I'll move in with Paisley for the rest of the week. It'll look like we're just two friends terrified for each other, right?"

Santiago sat back. "I was hoping you'd suggest that, Mika. I think that's a great idea, but again, neither of you have to do anything more if you're uncomfortable. If you stop showing interest, they will leave you alone in a few days – at least, I think so."

I sighed. "We really started something here, didn't we?"

"I'm afraid so, but to be honest, I didn't think they'd take it this far. I'm surprised by the surveillance."

I studied Santiago's face, and I could see the lines that made his face so handsome were a little deeper than usual. He was worried. "Should we be worried?"

He put his hands behind his head and looked at the ceiling. "I really don't know. But I want the two of you to be together as much as possible, and when you can't, you need to let me know by text, okay?"

Both Mika and I nodded. "Okay, what's your schedule for the next couple of days?" I said to Mika.

Mika ran through her days with us. She'd be in the store tomorrow and Saturday and said I could always be here. I started to say that sounded like a good plan, that I could get some research done if she didn't mind Sawyer spending Friday with us in the store, when my phone rang.

"Hi Saul. What's up?"

"The house site is clear. Ready to get to work tomorrow?" He sounded downright tickled with the idea, and to be honest, I was kind of excited myself. A distraction felt like a great idea.

"Um, I need to work out childcare for tomorrow, but if I can do that, then yes. Get back to you in fifteen?"

"Sounds good." He hung up without another word.

"Tomorrow's a go at the house." I tried to look somber because this was a scary moment, but I wasn't sure the relief of renewed income and expectation about a day of productivity stayed off my face.

"I wondered when he'd call. I let him know the site was no longer a crime scene just before I came over. He works fast." Santiago scratched his chin. "If I can get Sawyer an on-site sitter, would that help?"

I sat forward. "It would. What do you have in mind?"

"Me," he said with a grin. "I can keep an eye on you and also keep Sawyer busy. I'll just play it off that it's about the body and police business. What do you think?"

I thought for a second and realized that might be the ideal plan. No one would doubt that he was there just in case more bones turned up, and he'd be the ideal protection for Sawyer, and the rest of us, if we needed it. "Works for me," I said and felt a little shiver of excitement at getting to see Santiago with my son again. "You don't think they'll be suspicious?"

Santiago shrugged. "I don't think so, but we need to keep both of you safe. And Sawyer too." He looked from me to Mika. "Mika, I'll have officers in plain clothes in your store at all times tomorrow. We're doing a little trade of personnel with the Orange police for the next few days. They should be folks who aren't as easily ID'd as my deputies."

"Man, you *are* worried," I whispered.

"Cults are not small-time stuff, and with a body involved . . ."

"So you do think Rocket's death has something to do with Mountain Green!" Mika squealed before slapping her hand over her mouth in surprise at her own volume. "Sorry," she said quietly.

"In a place as small as our town, I don't leave much to coincidence, not when a murder is involved." The sheriff tugged his cap low on his head as he stood.

I stood beside him and started to walk him to the door before I remembered the people watching us.

"I'll be heading out now. I know I mentioned cider and donuts today. Why don't you and Sawyer swing by, but get him to suggest it when you get outside?" He looked at me. "Will he do that?"

"Shout something loudly about sweets? Yes, he can do that." I smiled, but I really just wanted to take my little boy to a bunker somewhere and hole up. "We'll come by for a few minutes."

"I won't be able to talk to you there, but text me when you get home, okay? And you're not to be alone, alright? Neither of you." He turned and held my gaze.

It took me a few minutes to gather my thoughts and corral a toddler, but when I mentioned donuts and police cars, I had to lunge after him to keep him from running outside and into the street on his own. As I shoved his arms into his coat and squeezed him so I could zip it up, I whispered, "When you get outside, I want you to shout, "Donuts!" as loudly as you can, okay?"

He looked up at me and said, "Okay, Mama. I shout."

I kissed his forehead. "You ready?"

"Ready!" he shouted into my face. Then we were off. Two

steps out the door, and he screamed, "DONUTS!" like he was letting the entire county know. I held his hand and half-ran, half-walked to the police station up the street. The boy was excited.

As we got closer, I slowed down both because Sawyer found groups of kids intimidating at first and because I wanted to see if I could get a read on whether or not anyone was following us. He and I walked to the edge of the crowd milling around a folding table on the sidewalk in front of the police station, and I turned to look behind me. Sure enough, about a block back, Santa Man and some other fellow in dungarees and plaid were strolling along.

I tried to let my eyes skim past them like it was no big deal, but Santa Man met my gaze and smiled just slightly. My stomach lurched. They didn't care at all that I knew, and that made me even more terrified.

I turned back to Sawyer, bent down to his ear and said, "Ready for a donut?"

His eyes were wide as he studied the children around him. "Pick me up?"

Normally, I tried to not carry him much because he was old enough to walk easily and because my middle-aged hips didn't love the imbalance carrying him caused, but today, I did so eagerly. With him scooped tight in my arms and his head on my shoulder so he could see but also feel secure, we waded into the crowd.

Officer Winslow looked up and said, "Well, look at this future schoolkid! Little guy, do you want a donut?"

Sawyer looked at the fried dough in her hand and nodded. She stood and handed him the food before meeting my eyes just an extra second and smiling. Just that small gaze of knowing opened up a well of peace in my chest. I smiled back before turning and wandering out of the bustling group of waist-high bodies around me.

Once we were clear, Sawyer began chowing down on his doughnut, and I started to slide him down off my body. But then, I saw Santa Man and his friend standing at the edge of the sidewalk between us and Mika's store. They were clearly waiting for us, so I hugged Sawyer tighter and walked toward them, trying to look both innocent and shy. Since I was neither, this was tough.

A few steps before we reached them, Santa Man stepped out and said, "Nice to see you out and about, Paisley. You've been holed up in that store for hours. We all need fresh air from time to time."

I took a slow, deep breath as Sawyer latched onto my waist with his knees. He was scared, too. "Well, we heard there were doughnuts."

"That is exciting," Santa Man said and reached toward Sawyer's back as if to rub it.

I turned my son away. I would play the part and try not to punch this guy, but I drew the line at strangers touching my son without his permission.

Santa Man frowned as he pulled his hand back, but I didn't care. "There are more if you guys want some?" I smiled weakly, just so eager to get this conversation over with.

"No, thank you. We'll leave them for people who need them more." Santa Man looked at me a minute. "Good choice to just let the kid have one, though. Probably don't need to add to those good child-bearing hips you have anyway."

I clenched my teeth and cleared my throat as color flooded my face. I had about a million cutting things to say in response, but I held my tongue and let them think, as I knew they would, that my blush was because I was embarrassed about my weight. I wasn't. I liked my body the way it was.

"Good to see you, Ms. Sutton," Santa Man said. Then, he stepped back and let us pass.

I walked as quickly as I could with fear, rage, and a toddler weighing me down, but when I was back in Mika's shop, I carried Sawyer to Ms. Stephenson and said, "I need a minute. Do you mind?"

She took one look at my face and said, "No, dear. We'll be right here with Sawyer's donut and cat's cradle." She took a small partial skein of yarn and began to show Saw how to weave it around her fingers to play the old-fashioned game.

I kissed my son on the cheek, turned away, and let the tears fall. Then, I went to the storeroom where Mika was surveying her inventory for her next order, put my head into a big bin of yarn, and screamed.

It only took me a minute to explain what had happened to Mika and to pull myself together. But man, I was angry. No one talked to me like that, especially in front of my son.

"I'm texting Santiago," she said.

I nodded. "Then you ready to go?"

"Yep. Definitely closing a bit early today." She took out her phone, tapped out the text, and then slipped her arm through mine. "Let's go."

Within a half-hour, we had seen Ms. S. safely to her car, using the premise that she had to carry a lot of yarn for her knitting circle that was making socks for homeless people, and the three of us were on our way up to Mika's apartment to pack a bag. Saw loved visiting Mika's place because it was full of cool things like antique fence pullers that appeared to be tugging colorful silk yarn into a spider's web, and she let him play with anything. To her credit, she did always look at me for my nod before saying yes when he asked to touch something, but my basic rule was that if it couldn't maim my son and the owner of said item didn't care, then it was a yes.

While Mika packed her bag, Sawyer investigated bowling by tossing a big ball of yarn at the antique bowling pins Mika had set up in the corner of her living room. The racket was enough to make me want to pull my hair out, but he was occupied and doing minimal damage. I plugged my ears with my fingers and waited.

Fortunately, Mika was a minimalist in terms of clothes, meaning she wore roughly the same outfit every day – jeans and a button-down shirt in one of various colors. It was her accessories that set each look apart. She had the best scarves, earrings, and headwraps, and she was fearless about wearing any of them. One day, I had walked into the store to find her in dark-wash jeans, a hot pink shirt, and a jungle-printed scarf that she had wrapped around her hair like a bandana with long tails running down her back. Her tiger earrings and giraffe necklace gave the whole outfit just the right bit of humor, and she looked amazing. I would have been too uneasy to even try the scarf, let alone the jewelry.

But this simple system of clothes meant she was done packing in five minutes, just as Sawyer discovered the antique spyglass she'd found at a flea market when we were in college. It would not have fared well in Sawyer's hands, and Mika would not have cared. But I would have.

The two of us let Sawyer bounce between us and out the door, where Mika locked up and put up a sign on the shop door saying, "See you tomorrow at nine a.m. sharp." She wasn't going to have many customers on a Friday evening in the winter, but she wanted to be sure she let them know she'd be open as usual the next day. Smart businesswoman.

My car was right outside at the curb, but I made a point of walking around the front of the car as I went to help Sawyer into his car seat from the street side. That's when I saw the two men, not men I recognized but clearly men watching me, in a pickup truck just a little bit up and across the road. Again, they didn't even try to hide that they were watching when I looked right at them, and I had to resist the temptation to give them a certain-fingered salute. But instead, I ducked my head and climbed into the driver's seat. Just had to keep this meek and mild cover going for three more days.

We swung by the local pizza place for a large with extra cheese and pepperoni and a two-liter of Cheerwine because there was no way I was cooking tonight, not with Saw all hopped up on Auntie Mickie. When we told him that she was going to stay with us and sleep in his bed for a few nights, he pumped his tiny fists and said, "Yeah." And then, for the entire ride to the pizza parlor and then home, he reviewed what he and Auntie Mickie were going to do tonight. She agreed to everything, including a makeup session, and I enjoyed seeing her delight. I was also glad I had two cans of apple pie cider for us to enjoy after he went to sleep because this boy had a full agenda planned.

Fortunately, Sawyer spent most of his energy showing Mika how fast he could run from tree to tree in the farmhouse yard, and by the time he'd eaten two gigantic pieces of pizza, sipped a tiny bit of watered-down soda, and had a bath, he was ready to show Mika the joys of *PJ Masks*.

The day had been full of goodness and activity, and that boy, for the first time in his life, fell asleep in front of the TV. It had been something I'd hoped for many times, for my sake but also for his. I had wonderful memories of dozing off watching a movie and having one of my parents carry me to my room in a half-waking state. Somehow, those moments always just felt very safe.

Now, for the first time, I got to do that with my little man, and I was a little teary from the tenderness of the moment after the scariness of the day. Fortunately, he just let himself be picked up, and when I tucked him in and told him, "I love you," he snuggled deeper under the covers of my bed. It was adorable . . . and so appreciated because I really wanted that cider and a chance to talk with Mika about everything.

She was my closest friend for a reason, and when I came back downstairs from tucking Sawyer in, she had the ciders open alongside a plate of peanut butter saltines and the last of my Girl Scout Cookie stash from the freezer. Thin Mints are always better frozen.

We sat on the floor by the fireplace and pretended we were at a college bonfire out on Starry Field, the athletic campus at our small Pennsylvania college. Both of us had been bookish and artsy in college, where being the most "holy" or the most athletic was the way to popularity, so those bonfires had been a social torture. But we still went, hoping to figure out how we fit in, and eventually we did, when we found our other artsy friends who wanted to sneak to a diner at eleven p.m. and smoke and drink coffee while pretending to do our homework.

Now, fully settled in ourselves and in our forties, the two of us made up the core of our social circle, and as best I could tell, she loved it as much as I did. I knew she'd like to meet someone special, and I wanted that for her, too, but for now, we were happy being the two of us. That was another reason I was hesitant about starting something with Santiago. I didn't want to disrupt my friendship with Mika in any way.

But that was a consideration for another time when the same pickup truck wasn't driving up and over the railroad bridge every hour. My farmhouse is on a quiet road, and vehicles have to slow way down just at the end of my driveway to make a ninety-degree turn. So I had gotten a peek at the truck several times as it went by. I didn't know if it was the same guys inside, but someone was definitely making sure we were staying in.

"So they could think we are lesbians, you know?" Mika said with a smile.

"They could. They wouldn't be the first to think so, and they won't be the last." For years, people had assumed Mika and I were a couple, and neither of us minded. We were both pretty far over on the straight side of the sexual orientation spectrum, but it wasn't an insult for people to think we were together. I took it as a compliment, in fact. Mika was gorgeous, and any woman or man would be lucky to have her.

"They won't, though," she continued, "because that's so far off their narrow-minded, backwards trail of thought that it wouldn't even occur to them to consider it."

"We could go outside on the porch under the light and kiss if you want," I said with a wry grin.

"It has been a while since I've had a good snog, but no thanks." Mika laughed. "Seriously, though, it's very creepy that they're watching us."

I sighed. "It is. I guess I kind of understood that they might follow us into town just to be sure we weren't lying about the sheriff. Although, come to think of it, we might have been his spies reporting back." I leaned back on my elbows and immediately regretted it when the ache started immediately in my neck. I couldn't relive too much of those college years in this middle-aged body anymore. "But they must be hard-core or very interested in recruiting us if they are working this hard."

"Do you really think they might recruit us?"

"You didn't get the 'college tour' feel today? If Reverend Villay had started walking backwards while he talked, I would have begun considering what my major would be."

Mika spit cider into the gas fireplace when she laughed. "Oh my goodness, I remember when I had to learn to navigate the entire campus backwards just so I didn't turn my back on the prospective students and their parents. My calves were amazing."

I smiled. "You were a great guide, I bet. Did you tell them there were ghosts in Old Main?" Old Main was the administrative building on campus, and it housed faculty offices, too. A lot of us teased the very earnest freshmen about the ghosts of the school's founding fathers who haunted the building looking for their errant wives who had decided to play gin rummy. Our alma mater had been very conservative at one time, and some of the students still thought playing cards was the devil's work. The first year Mika and I were there was the first year students were actually allowed to dance on campus.

"Every time," Mika said. "I'd walk them past the registrar and say, 'You won't hear this on other tours, but people say that a man in suspenders and a straw hat walks these halls at night calling, "Elizabeth, Elizabeth, did you iron my work pants?' They'd look at me with a little suspicion until I said, 'The first president of Messiah was S.R. Smith.' I'd pause here for effect before I said, 'His wife's name was Elizabeth.'"

"You did not?" I said. This was the first time I'd heard this story, although we'd joked for years about the scandal it would cause if, indeed, a ghost tried to haunt that Christian campus. It would have been prayed into heaven by sundown.

"I did, and every time, some tiny young woman in the back would squeal and be immediately comforted by a boy on the tour. By the third week of the semester, I'd see them macking it up in the dining hall." She rolled her eyes.

Our college also didn't allow men or women in each other's rooms, so a lot of those hormones got brought to the dining room, the doorways outside the dorms, or the library. All that making out was just icky.

"Maybe that's how we get out of this Mountain Green thing on Sunday if it goes sideways. We tell them we see dead people." I held Mika's gaze until I couldn't suppress my laughter any longer.

Mika snickered and said, "I'll be sure to look up who the first pastor was and find out his wife's name. The same story should work here."

I snorted with laughter and felt just a tiny bit of the tension of the day fall aside. "I can't believe we actually drove up there like that. What were we thinking?"

Mika's face grew very serious. "We were thinking that women are being attacked, and we needed to do something about it."

I pursed my lips and nodded. "You're right. So let's figure out our next steps. I don't think we can really do anything until Sunday, do you?"

"I've been thinking about that, actually. If I'm remembering correctly, and I think I am, Marge may be in this weekend. She seems to come by near the end of each month, maybe because she gets some sort of allowance or something." Mika shivered. "If her routine holds, she might be coming in this weekend, and even if she wasn't planning on it, I expect the men at Mountain Green want to send her in just to get a bead on what exactly I'm thinking."

"So you're thinking you might be able to turn the tables on them? Maybe Marge would help?" I sat up straight again and leaned forward to stretch my back and to see Mika's expression more clearly in the firelight.

"I'm not sure. I don't want to put her in danger, and if she's not willing to help, I might put us in danger by telling her our plan. I was more thinking about just asking her some questions, seeing what she'd tell me if I seemed sincere." Mika rubbed the back of her neck. "I hate to deceive her, though."

I sighed. "Yeah, I don't like that either, but it would probably be better if she could report back that you just asked the kind of questions they'd expect."

"And what would those questions be? I guess I need to get into character more."

I stood up and stretched before going to my desk and getting a pen and paper. "Let's make a list."

We spent the next half-hour trying to remember what we'd wanted to know about college as high school seniors because that was as close an experience to joining a cult as we could think of. Actually, there turned out to be a surprising amount of relevance, which made me think I'd need to revisit my memories of college with a more critical eye sometime soon.

But for now, we had a solid plan for Mika, and if Marge came in on Saturday when I'd be there, then I could talk with her, too, if she didn't seem put off by that.

By ten p.m., Mika and I were spent. I grabbed an extra blanket out of the cedar chest for Mika to use on Sawyer's bed and wished her sweet space dreams under his rocket sheets before I climbed into bed next to my adorable boy, who I prayed would not be affected by any of his mama's shenanigans.

9

My alarm went off far too early. Fortunately, Sawyer was already stirring, so I didn't have to tend to a sobbing child whose waking had come on too harshly. Instead, he looked at me and said, "What we doing today, Mama?"

I groaned, sat up, and said, "Want to go watch some big equipment?"

He was out of bed and heading downstairs before I even got my feet on the floor. That child could name every piece of digging machinery out there, and heaven forbid I should call a front-end loader a bulldozer. He was not shy about correcting my terminology, not one bit.

Mika stood at the door of his room and mumbled something about dreaming she'd gone to the moon with Elon Musk. I patted her on the shoulder as I stepped past her to get the clothes I'd laid out for Sawyer the night before and followed my son downstairs.

Saw's enthusiasm had waned just a little bit when he realized it was still dark outside, but once I got the lights in the house on and the fire going, he began his long list of questions, all of which I quelled with an upraised hand and two words: Mama's Coffee.

He sat down on the couch with his baby doll and giant teddy bear and watched the fire. The boy was young but he understood, already, my need for caffeine.

The kettle going for the French press, I fixed Sawyer a cup of chocolate milk, his morning staple of quick calories, steeped my coffee, and sat down beside him to try and answer his barrage. "Will there be excavators?" "Can I sit on them?" "Will they be loud?" I had answers to most things, surprisingly. Satisfied, Sawyer took my phone and watched some videos while I finished the coffee and put on enough bacon for three of us.

A few minutes later, Sawyer was dressed, the cream of wheat and bacon were done, and we were all eating well, even Sawyer who wanted to eat Mika's food instead of his own. Smart Auntie let him and then scooped up his plate to down enough calories for her own day.

A few minutes later with everyone, including the cat, fed and dressed (Beau insisted on coming, so he was wearing his harness), we piled back into my car and headed over the hills into town. I dropped Mika off early but was glad to see the patrol car parked nearby, a quick response to my "heading out" text to Santiago a few minutes prior.

Then, Sawyer, Beauregard, and I went on over to the demolition site and, hopefully, a few hours' work to secure us money for this month's bills. I was squeaking by, but barely, and I could really use the kind of quick cash that a couple of really stellar house beams would bring. I just hoped I wouldn't have to chop them up into mantels to sell them. It would be a shame to cut up wood that had survived intact for hundreds of years already.

At seven sharp, all of us convened at the house, Santiago included. He was in full uniform and driving his patrol car, so there was nothing subtle about his presence. "Someone definitely followed you here, Paisley, so don't go disappearing from the group today, okay?"

I blushed. I'd wandered off once before when I was under Santiago's watch, and it hadn't gone well. "I won't. You sure you're okay with this guy?" I said to Sawyer as I tried to look chagrined rather than giddy at the sight of this handsome man, just in case anyone was watching.

"He's okay," Sawyer said.

I rolled my eyes at my son, who grinned and, I was pretty sure, tried to wink at me, and then I turned back to the farmhouse and took a breath. The building must have been quite the looker in her day. Two stories with stone chimneys at either end. It was what I called a "two over two," which may be a technical term for a house with two rooms upstairs and two rooms down, but I had no idea if anyone but me used it. Each of the four rooms had a fireplace, since that would have been the only heat at the time, and while each room also had a window, they were small to conserve heat and keep the summer sun to a minimum.

At some point, a more recent owner had put on an addition at the back with a kitchen and bathroom, but those had long ago succumbed to honeysuckle and maple seedlings. Modern construction techniques just don't stand up like the old ways, and you could really see it in a building like this.

I could have studied the façade of the house all day, but after only a few seconds, a shrill whistle brought my attention to Saul, who was at the side of the house and looking vastly impatient. I grimaced, slipped on my hard hat, and followed him to the back of the building. "I decided we'd start here," he said as I rushed up. He pointed to the back wall. "We can take off the roof here, and probably save some of this wood for your art projects or whatever."

Saul appreciated architectural salvage for the big stuff – the old trees turned into buildings, especially – but if the wood had paint on it, he wasn't interested. "Ruined a perfectly good piece of lumber," he'd say. For the most part, I agreed with him, but there was a big market for what used to be called "shabby chic." Dad could make a lot of picture frames from this siding, and I could use the income those would bring. Plus, who wanted all this going into the landfill anyway?

"Sounds good. Did you notice if the roof beams were still sound?"

"You mean when I was crawling around risking life and limb to assure your payday?" he asked with a wink. "I sure did. They look pretty good. Mostly the roof sheeting that's rotted out. We'll get you some good pieces."

"Awesome. Let's get going then." I tried to sound authoritative, but I was really missing Mika's leadership right now. I knew, though, that she needed to be running her own business today. Still, I was missing her 3D renderings as I tried to do some quick mental math to figure out what kind of money I might recoup from this job.

I wanted to give Saul's guys something. I knew Saul wouldn't let me really pay them, but I was hoping Saul would let me cover the fuel costs for his equipment. I mentally tabulated the value of the beams, the doorframes, the hardware, the three mantels that were still intact enough to salvage, and the second-story floorboards that were still in good shape. I was terrible with numbers, especially without paper, but I thought I might be able to clear five thousand – even with tips and fuel costs. That would cover Sawyer and me for a month or more, and that would be amazing.

Just then, a giant green piece of equipment swung its arm over my head and lifted up the corner of the roof to my left. In one swift move that I couldn't have even managed with my own hand blown up to scale, the operator took the roof up. Then, he looked at me, and I stared at his very impressive beard. I was pretty sure it would touch his belt buckle when he stood up.

Only when Saul jerked me out of the way did I realize that the operator was waiting for me to move so that he didn't drop the entire roof on my head. I blushed what I knew must have been a ferocious shade of crimson and decided to take up a position further away from the work.

The morning's demolition went smoothly and landed me a bonus – the first story was actually an old log cabin that had just been clad with wood siding. Most of the logs were in great shape, so I had at least another five thousand in revenue there. Sawyer's college fund was actually going to get a contribution this month.

We had the first row of logs off and stacked on the flatbed that Saul had, with another stroke of generosity, called up when it became clear we weren't going to be able to fit everything in a couple of pickup trucks, and we decided to break for lunch.

Fortunately, I had managed to think ahead a little as I went to bed the night before and called a friend of a friend who owned the amazing Pie Guy food truck, and he was set up at the edge of the road when we came around the house. The men actually cheered because who doesn't love a homemade pastry full of hot meat and cheese.

I was glad they were happy, but I also knew that these guys could probably pack away some food. So I didn't shy away from jumping in line to get a bowl of mac and cheese for Sawyer and two pies for Santiago to pick from: chicken and mushroom and chicken coconut curry. I'd eaten every pie this guy offered, and they were all amazing. Once the crew realized how good the food was, the Pie Guy was going to sell out.

I acted nervous as I strolled over to the patrol car and offered up, with head down, my pies to Santiago. He covered up his laugh with a cough and then took one of the pies without asking any questions. I gathered Sawyer up after mumbling "thank you" and being sure the sheriff caught my wink and climbed into the hatch of my car for us to eat. It wouldn't do for me to seem too friendly with law enforcement, I figured. They might understand how a "weak" woman like myself had to rely on free childcare, but they wouldn't understand small talk with the enemy.

Sawyer, hungry from his cavorting in a police car, scarfed down his macaroni and half of my pie, which turned out to be the chicken and mushroom. I was glad I'd packed some goldfish and Z-bars, so I could get enough food for myself to make it through the afternoon. I was just swallowing the last of the juice box when the brown pickup I'd been seeing everywhere pulled up next t+o the sheriff's car.

Santiago threw me a glance to let me know he understood and then proceeded to walk casually our way with trash in hand as if he needed a place to throw it away. I debated putting Sawyer right into his car seat so we could make a quick getaway, but I figured I couldn't do that quickly enough to be worth the attention it would draw. So I settled for snuggling him close while he watched some videos. Dad was going to be here soon to take him for his ride and nap, and I couldn't decide if I wanted him to come now or stay away so he wasn't in danger.

I was still considering my best course of action when Saul walked over to the truck, shook the driver's hand, and then struck up a lengthy, laughter-filled conversation with the driver. I couldn't see the person's face, but to me, it looked like he and Saul had known each other a long, long time. I wasn't sure if that was a good thing or a very, very bad one.

Sawyer remained oblivious to my tension, but the sheriff was not. Santiago was inching closer and closer to the car as he pretended to talk on the phone, and every few moments, he caught my eye and gave me a long stare as if to say, "Stay calm, Paisley. Stay calm."

I tried to take a few deep breaths and not crane my neck too much to see if I could get a peek at the pickup driver's face, but when none of that worked, I watched Saw's videos with him and found the antics of tiny animated pandas were, indeed, good distraction.

Eventually, though, I couldn't pretend any longer because Saul called my name and said, "Paisley, come meet someone." He was still standing by the truck. My heart dropped into my ankles.

I squeezed Sawyer tight and told him that he was going into the car cave. Then, I lowered the hatch and locked the door, dropping my keys below the bumper when I saw Santiago watching. He gave me a tiny nod to show he understood, and then I walked toward the truck.

Saul looked completely like his normal, easygoing self, and I tried to focus on my longtime friend as I approached the truck that had been terrifying me for two days now. The man inside stepped out, and I was face-to-face, again, with Santa Man. Only then did I realize I'd been harboring some small hope that the truck was a look-alike and not related to this wild ride of a cult-infiltration that I'd gotten myself on.

"Paisley, meet Nicholas Sterit. He's an old friend. Nick, this here is Ms. Paisley Sutton, the fine leader of our activities today." Saul patted me on the shoulder with pride.

I tried to smile, but I'm pretty sure I just stared because it felt like my cover had been blown. A woman who leads a group of men in a salvage job does not try to join a cult where the women are, in every way, considered servants to the men.

"Oh, Saul, Paisley and I met just a couple of days ago up in the Hollow," Nick said with a smile. "She and her friend Mika came by."

A flash of something I couldn't read flickered across Saul's face, but then, he smiled and said, "That so, Nick? Well, you do have a mighty fine piece of beauty up there. That's for sure."

"Sure do. And it's kind of you to help Paisley out like this. I see all your equipment and your crew. Mighty kind of you," Santa Man said with approval.

Just then, I understood something very key about men who really hate women. They take pleasure in pretending to elevate us, and that's exactly what he thought Saul was doing, pretending. He didn't think I was running this operation because I couldn't be. Saul had to be in charge. Again, I wished Mika were here with her work plans and sketches just to drive home the point that women could, indeed, do anything.

My next disturbing realization was that, maybe, Saul wasn't exactly who I thought he was. How could he be friends with someone like Santa Man? Didn't he know about the way women were treated at Mountain Green? Didn't he care?

"Nice to see you again, Mr. Sterit," I said quietly. This time, I wasn't faking anything. I was feeling completely thrown off, and the "Mr. Sterit" part just came naturally after years of manners training from my parents. If someone was older than you, you called them Mr., Mrs., Ms., or Miss unless they told you otherwise, even if they were terrorizing you and your loved ones.

"I've been seeing you around, Paisley," Nick said, "and I like what I see. You're a good friend to Mika, and you take good care of that fine son of yours."

My heart had started to race the second he laid out that he had, indeed, been following me, but when he brought up Sawyer, a surge of adrenaline so strong nearly had me lunging toward him across the gravel between us. There was no doubt he was putting me on notice that I was being watched and that they knew I had a little boy to keep safe.

I couldn't think of anything but swear words to say. I just nodded and stared at my feet so that I didn't give into the temptation to grab Santa Man's white beard and use it to fling his head against his truck door.

Saul kicked some rocks at his feet, and the small movement

got my attention and made me look up. He met my gaze and said, "Thanks for coming over to say hi. I know Sawyer's waiting. We'll get started again in a few minutes, shall we?"

I nodded and mumbled, "Nice to see you again," before walking to my car. At the back, I feigned straightening my pants cuff in my work boots so that I could get my keys and take a few deep breaths before opening the door to my son, who did not need to know his mother was terrified.

Sawyer's videos had just ended, and he was busy climbing around the car and pushing every button in sight. I grabbed for the phone on the floor and texted Santiago as quickly as I could.

Nicholas Sterit. He's the man who's been following me.

I know. Ran his plates. Same one that's been by Mika's shop and your house the past couple of days. Registered to him at an address up in the Hollow.

He threatened me.

I could see Santiago out the window of the car, and when he read that text, he started toward me.

No. It was subtle. Nothing I could report officially. I'm okay. Sawyer is okay.

You can stop this at any time, remember.

Not now. Not after that. Also, Saul knows him.

I saw that, too.

He shook his head and put his phone in his back pocket as Saul headed toward the back of my car.

"You were up at Mountain Green, huh? Thinking of taking up a more submissive life?"

Saul was smiling, but there was something hard in his eyes. I couldn't read it, and after that long conversation he'd had with Santa Man, I didn't know what to make of his attitude about Reverend Villay's church. So I simply said, "It's hard being a single mom. Sometimes it feels like it would be really nice to have a whole lot of people around to help."

That was total truth and something I'd thought many times. But Saul didn't need to know that I would no more take my son to that horrible place than I would tell him that it was okay to hit a woman.

"You just be sure about what you're getting into there, Paisley. The church doesn't take kindly to looky-loos." Saul turned and walked away, and I couldn't tell if I'd just been given a kind warning or another threat.

I MADE it through the next few hours in a daze. The logs came down, and we got not just three but all four mantels off the walls. Saul also had the guys load up a pallet of chimney stones for me and said he had a buyer for those. They were going to hire Saul and his crew to make a firepit at their old farmhouse. If it hadn't been for the whole cult thing and the fact that one of the men I most respected might be a supporter of theirs, it would have been a good day.

When we were done, I gathered up all of Sawyer's snack wrappers and took off my work boots before getting into the car to go and pick up Sawyer from Dad's house. Dad had come just after we resumed work, and Sawyer had been cooked. The transition had been quick and easy, and when Sawyer had said he wanted to come back and watch the big equipment some more, I said a firm no. I just couldn't risk having him near anyone. I'd told Dad to take him home with him and keep him in the backyard only, and Dad had raised an eyebrow but thankfully hadn't asked any questions.

Now, I needed to explain the situation before I arrived so that I could get Sawyer into the car in time to pick Mika up when she closed the shop. I didn't want her there after dark, even if a police officer would be nearby.

Lucille answered on the first ring and said, "Your dad said you looked worried. What's going on?"

"I don't have time to do more than tell you right now, okay?" My stepmother and I could talk for hours if we didn't have demands on our time, so I needed to make it clear that my time was short.

"Okay, talk fast then." Lucille sounded both concerned and interested.

I told her about the potential link between Rocket's murder and Mountain Green Church. Then, I told her about Mika and me visiting the Hollow, and the other end of the line went very, very quiet.

"Go on," she said.

"Now, we're being watched, and Mika is staying with me. We have police officers checking on us, and we are safe. But one of the men from there came to the job site today—"

Lucille interrupted me and said, "Okay, so here's what we're going to do. Your dad is going to come stay with you tonight. Sawyer is going to stay with me for his first sleepover with his Baba, and we're doing it in a hotel."

It took me a minute to process what she'd said, but when I did, I gasped with gratitude. Her plan was perfect, and to have my dad there at my house, well, that meant so much. But there was one problem. "Won't they get suspicious if my dad is there? Doesn't that seem weird?"

"A bunch of men who treat women like they do will think nothing at all odd about having a father watching over his daughter. It'll feel right and proper to them. They probably think you should have moved home after your divorce anyway." The disdain in Lucille's voice was palpable.

"Good point," I said. "But I have to take Sawyer to his dad's in the morning—"

She cut me off. "I'll take him. Your ex will just have to understand that you are not feeling well and that I needed to do drop-off for the weekend. See you in a few." She hung up, and I dropped the phone into my lap.

I drove the last few miles to their house in a sort of daze. I had done everything I knew to protect Sawyer, and still, I needed help to keep him safe. At my core, I felt like I was failing as a parent, but then I remembered what one of the women in a mom's group on Facebook had said just before Sawyer was born – "It's not a failure to ask for help. It's a failure to not ask and still need the help." So I gave myself a good pep talk just like I would to anyone else in my situation and reminded myself that I was doing a good job, a great job some days, and that I had people who wanted to help me.

By the time I pulled up at Dad and Lucille's house, I was feeling a bit better about myself but still nervous about what they might say. I took a second to text Sawyer's father and tell him I was under the weather and that Lucille would be bringing our son to him in the morning since he was staying the night there. He said, *Okay. Feel better*, in reply.

When I walked into the house, Sawyer plowed into my thighs and said, "Baba and I are going to a hotel with a pool!"

My eyebrows raised as I looked at his grandmother over my head. "The Omni downtown has an indoor pool, and we still have Sawyer's swimmies here. Plus, Sawyer, I just checked," she said as she turned to him, "and they have chicken nuggets *and* noodles in the restaurant. We can order them to our room after we swim and"—she paused here for dramatic effect, and Sawyer's eyes went as wide as dinner plates—"we can eat in bed."

Lucille knew how to create a magical adventure for my boy, and I was so grateful.

Sawyer looked back up at me and said, "Mommy, did you hear that? I get to eat noodles in bed."

"I did hear that, Little Man. That's going to be so much fun." I gave my stepmother a warm smile. "Do you have all your things ready to go?" I was not about to leave the two of them here without us, and so I was relieved to see that Lucille already had a bag packed with the extra clothes and diapers we kept at their house. Sawyer's Paw Patrol swim belt was sticking out of the top. "Thank you," I said as Sawyer went to hug his Boppy before he left.

"You are most welcome. It'll be an adventure for both of us." She peeked down the hall to be sure that Saw was out of earshot. "You're doing a good thing, Paisley. I've heard the stories from up there, too, and the sheriff filled your dad in when they spoke a few minutes ago."

I felt my eyebrows go up, and I wanted to interrupt and get that bit of information fleshed out, but I didn't. Lucille had something she needed to say, and the least I could do for all she was doing for me was to listen.

"But that little boy needs you, so don't do anything stupid, okay?" She hugged me close. "We need you, too."

I choked back my tears and said, "I know. And we've got a sound plan and lots of people watching out for us." I stood back and looked at her as I weighed whether I wanted to ask the next question. "Um, you don't think Saul could be mixed up in things up there, do you?"

"Our Saul?" She stared at me a minute. "I doubt it, but I've lived long enough to say that nothing surprises me. But I sure hope not."

Sawyer bounced back in and said, "I ready. Mommy, you ready?"

I knelt down and pulled my son close. "Mommy can't come, Love Bug. I have to stay home with Boppy and Auntie Mickie. But you and Baba are going to have a special night, just the two of you." I wanted to cry, and I really wanted to lay in a bed and eat macaroni and cheese and chicken nuggets. But neither of those was an option tonight.

Sawyer looked at me with a little sadness on his face, but then Baba swept in with a big hug and the promise of monster truck videos while they ate, and he was headed for the door without even a wave. I snuck up to the front of the house to be sure I didn't see any familiar vehicles, particularly a brown pickup, on the street. When it seemed the coast was clear, I gave the signal, and they ran to Lucille's car and loaded up. They were out and gone in three minutes flat, and I felt a little tension seep from my shoulders. I couldn't guarantee that they hadn't been seen, but I thought it unlikely.

Still, when Dad came up behind me, a duffel bag over his shoulder, he said, "Santiago has someone in the next room at the Omni. They're safe, Paisley."

I sagged back against him and let a couple of tears fall. "Thanks, Daddy. And thanks for coming to stay with us. I'll feel better with you there."

"You'll feel better? I wasn't going to sleep a wink with you out there alone. At least now, I won't miss out on my beauty rest."

I smiled. "And . . . you get to sleep under spaceships."

"Fly me to the moon," he sang as he guided me to the door.

10

Dad drove my car because we figured it best we play the roles to a T, and most men, at least the ones that I knew, prefer to be in control of the car. My dad was actually the opposite, but for the sake of appearances, he agreed this was our best choice.

There were two benefits of this situation. First, I could text Mika to find out if she thought Thai sounded good. Lucille had insisted we pick up dinner on the way home, and there was a great Thai place between us and her shop. She said yes immediately and requested her usual pad Thai, "extra mild," to which I sent the eye roll emoji because, seriously, the woman was a wimp when it came to spice.

The second advantage of having Dad drive was that his good ear was to the window, which made it hard to talk. I wanted to talk all this through with my dad, especially to find out why Santiago had called him – but first, I just needed a minute to gather my own thoughts, especially about Saul. Dad and Saul had known each other a long time, and Saul was Mika's uncle. I needed to know what I thought before I could talk to them about what they thought. So I pointed to the radio, and when Dad nodded, I found the oldies station and smiled while Dad sang along to every song. For a man of few words, he was also a man of many songs, as long as they had come out before 1970.

While Dad crooned away, I tried to make sense of the camaraderie between Santa Man and Saul. I knew that it was entirely possible that those two men had known each other since birth, secretly hated each other, but played nice in front of others. But I'd seen that with Dad and a couple of guys he'd grown up with – their repartee didn't include laughter. In fact, it couldn't even really be called *repartee*. More strictly speaking, they made small talk. But Saul and Santa Man? That was repartee at its best.

Saul was truly one of the best people I knew, and while he wasn't all up on the politically correct terms and sometimes made jokes with Dad about women in the kitchen, he also knew – as did Dad – that all such jokes were met with glares and far less attention from the women they were goading. So I couldn't get my mind around the idea that Saul would be friendly with a guy who was, obviously, some sort of upper echelon lackey of that Reverend Villay. He had to have heard the stories, too.

I decided, as best I could with my super-strong tendency to form opinions and then just deal with the consequences of them later, to wait to decide what I thought until I heard from Mika and Dad. Maybe I'd just missed something.

THE THAI FOOD was hot and ready when I ran in to get it, and I sent Lucille a text to say thank-you for dinner. She'd insisted on paying, and I was very grateful since funds were scarily low until I sold some of what we salvaged today.

As soon as we pulled up to Mika's shop, Mika and a woman I didn't recognize walked out of the store. The woman stood by, making small talk with Mika as she locked up. When the woman walked away, I saw a skein of pink yarn sticking out of her tote bag and smiled. Santiago and his team had thought of everything.

Mika slid into the seat behind me and said, "That was the longest day in the history of the world." As she slumped against the back of the seat, she sighed. Then, she sat forward with her chin on the shoulder of my seat and said, "That smells amazing."

"Doesn't it?" I gestured toward Dad's ear and said, "Tell us about your day when we get home?"

Mika nodded and then reached her head around to the other side of Dad's seat and said, "Hi, Mr. Sutton," into his good ear.

Dad reached a hand back and put his hand over hers. "Hey, Mika Girl. How are you?"

"Tired," she said and gave his fingers a squeeze before she sat back again. I turned partway back in my seat and said, "Was that one of the borrowed cops?"

"Yep. Officer Layton. She was this afternoon's guard – a great knitter, too. She was working up a baby sweater for her niece, and she taught me this new way to cast on—" She stopped herself and smiled. "Sorry, I forget you don't knit. Anyway, she sat in the window all afternoon and knitted."

"There was someone else there this morning?"

"Yep, Officer Davenport. He knitted, too, but he's just learning. Like *just* just learning. He picked it up for this situation. Said he wanted to look authentic."

"Good for him," I said. "More men should knit or crochet. Or even cross-stitch, for that matter. It would lower their blood pressure and make them . . ." I shot a look over at Dad, and even though I knew he probably couldn't hear me, I chose the kinder phrase. "Less mean."

"That's one term for what some men are," Mika said with a

sigh. "Marge did come in today, by the way. I'll tell you all about it when we get to your place."

We rode the rest of the way in silence – well, silence punctuated by Dad belting out "California Girls" like he was Brian Wilson's understudy. It was a good moment.

AT HOME, we set up tray tables in the living room, kicked up the fireplace, and proceeded to talk about the "security measures" Dad and Santiago had discussed on their phone call. The sheriff had reached out to suggest the plan that Lucille had just pitched to me, and Dad had been on board immediately. Though, he had warned Santiago that going around me to my father might have consequences. "I told him that he might get an earful about how you can take care of yourself."

I sighed. Dad wasn't wrong, but I decided to not engage with that particular part of the conversation, mostly because I was already exhausted.

Dad had checked all the doors and windows to be sure they were locked, which I figured would buy us three seconds if someone wanted in. Glass was pretty easy to get through, after all, but I didn't point that out.

Next, he wanted us to know he'd brought something to protect us. "Now, don't be worried. I do know how to use it." From behind the pillow beside him on the couch, he pulled out a black pistol, and I dropped my fork.

"Dad, you brought a gun? You know how I feel about those things!" I understood guns. Even knew how to shoot shotguns and rifles, but I loathed them. I had a rule about no guns in my house, especially with Sawyer there.

"Don't worry, honey," he said. "I know how to use it. Then, he pointed it at the fireplace and pulled the trigger.

I gasped and braced for the sound as my father discharged a gun in my living room, but all I heard was a little sizzle when the stream of water hit the flames. It was a water gun. "Dad, you scared the life out of me!"

The grin on my father's face was priceless. "Got you," he said, and he sounded just like his grandson. Then, his face grew more serious. "But you are keeping this by your bed. It might just buy us a few minutes if we need it. I have my shotgun here, too, the real one."

I wanted to protest, but honestly, given how brazen these Mountain Green people had been, I wasn't sure having a gun on hand was a bad idea, especially since Dad knew how to use it and wouldn't hesitate to do so if necessary.

"Don't those toy guns usually have orange tips on them or something?" Mika asked with a worried glance at me. She knew how guns made me feel.

"I took it off to make it look more authentic." Dad swallowed a big sip of his iced tea. "Now, let's talk about our plan if someone comes here."

By the time Dad had laid out the logistics of escape from upstairs if someone came in – a plan I insisted include Beauregard – I was exhausted and even more terrified than I had been. But I was grateful for the plan even as I hoped we wouldn't have to use it.

After our talk, I cleaned up the plates, and Mika started to browse Netflix for something we could all enjoy. It was going to take her a while to find something that fit the bill, I was sure, so I took that opportunity to say, "Saul and Santa Man were talking at the job site today."

Mika put down the remote and looked at me. "They were?"

"Who's Santa Man?" Dad said.

"His name is Nicholas Sterit," I said. "He came to the house where we were working today, and if I didn't know better, I'd say he and Saul were friends."

Mika opened her mouth to speak, but Dad didn't notice and

said, “They are friends. We’ve all known each other since kindergarten.”

I stared at my father, who was carefully studying each of the thumbnails on the screen and was oblivious to my shock. “Dad, Nick Sterit lives up at Mountain Green. He’s one of the guards who greeted us there yesterday.”

Dad’s eyes snapped to my face, and then he looked over at Mika. She nodded, but slowly. “So he and Uncle Saul are friends? Like real friends?” She pulled her eyes up from the trunk in front of the couch and turned to Dad beside her.

“We all got breakfast together on Saturday mornings for years. Nick is a good guy.” Dad frowned. “Maybe *was* is a better term here. I didn’t know he was living up there. Maybe Saul didn’t either?”

Dad looked from Mika to me. I sighed. “Maybe, but I think we have to ask, Miks, don’t you?”

Mika didn’t respond, and from the way she was staring into the dark kitchen beyond Dad, I wasn’t sure she was even with us in this conversation any more. “Mika?”

She shook her head and looked back at me. “Sorry. I was just thinking about something Uncle Saul said the day we found Rocket’s body.” She swallowed hard and then looked at me. “He said, ‘At least we were the ones to find him.’”

Dad huffed. “What’s wrong with that? Better for kind people who would care for the body and try to figure out who he was to dig him up than people who would just rebury him and never say a thing.”

“That’s what I thought at first, too,” Mika said, “but it was the way he said it. It’s been bugging me. It felt like maybe he knew something more about Rocket’s death, like he wasn’t telling me everything.”

I sank back into my grandfather’s leather armchair and took a deep breath. “You think Saul knew Rocket’s body was there all along?”

Mika looked up at me. "I don't know if I'd go that far, but it does seem weird that Saul was so readily available to help, not once but twice now."

"He said it was slow because of the holidays." Even I realized that sounded kind of lame in retrospect.

Dad stood up and said, "I'm calling Saul."

Mika and I lunged at him as he pulled his phone from his pocket, but he just walked out of the room and dialed.

I moved over to sit with Mika on the couch and pulled out the quilt I'd snuggled under when I was sick as a child. I laid it over our laps and said, "Why does this keep getting harder and harder?"

Mika groaned and said, "I don't know, but this sucks." She picked up the remote and clicked on *Marvelous Mrs. Maisel.* It was a good choice. We all needed a strong woman who didn't take anyone's crap.

A few minutes into the show, Dad came back in, and Mika hit pause. "Well?" she said.

Dad dropped into the rocking chair by the fireplace and said, "I don't know."

"What do you mean you don't know?" My voice was a little shrill, and I tried to back off a bit. "What does that mean, Daddy?"

"I thought Saul would tell me something that explained everything, but all he'd say is that we've known Nick a long time and that maybe he knew how to take care of you better than I did and definitely better than you two could take care of yourself." Dad's voice was quiet, but I could hear the ire behind it.

"Saul said that?" Mika's voice broke as she began to cry. "About me?"

I pulled my friend tight to my chest. And we thought it couldn't get worse.

. . .

None of us had felt much like watching TV or talking or anything after that, but we made ourselves sit through the rest of an episode of *Marvelous Mrs. Maisel*, which was an exercise in torture strong enough to distract all of us into sleep. You'd think I would have learned from the incident with *Clerks* when I was in college, but apparently not. Given the amount of shifting and throat-clearing that all three of us were doing during her Mrs. Maisel's first stand-up set, I think I can say that we were all, without a doubt, profoundly uncomfortable. Nothing like watching really funny – but also kind of crass – stand-up comedy with your dad.

Still, it got my mind off Saul and Mountain Green and all the other stuff . . . and fortunately, Mika doesn't insist on putting her cold feet against my back while she sleeps like Sawyer does. So I got a pretty good night's sleep. When the alarm went off at seven-thirty, I woke to the smell of coffee and bacon. I was confused and thought, for a minute, that maybe I'd been sleepwalking and prepared breakfast already.

But when I wandered down the stairs and into the kitchen, Dad was at the stove with an entire pound of bacon on the griddle and a pan of scrambled eggs cooking beside him. The French press was full, and I almost cheered with joy. Mostly my glee came from the fact that someone else was cooking, but coffee and bacon are also two of my favorite things in the world. I slid onto a stool by the kitchen peninsula and didn't even offer to help. I was going to relish this moment.

Dad smiled at me, poured me a cup of coffee, added a fair dollop of the one treat I always kept on hand for myself – Sweet Cream coffee creamer – and handed me a mug that Mika had made back in her pottery-throwing days in college. "Thank you so much," I said and took a long, slow sip. I was going to drink this whole cup of coffee while it was hot, and I was going to treasure that privilege.

My phone vibrated from the pocket of the comfy, washable

sweater I kept for mornings when the farmhouse could be three distinct climates. It was Lucille.

Sawyer just woke up after sleeping for twelve solid hours. He had a blast swimming and ate an entire grilled cheese sandwich, order of fries, and serving of broccoli.

Holy cow! No nuggets? Way to go! How long did he swim last night?

Two hours. He fell asleep with a french fry in his mouth.

Ha! Perfect. Did you sleep?

I did . . . but he did insist on putting his feet in the small of my back all night.

Every night. Thanks for taking toddler toes for the team. Headed to Mika's shop at nine.

I'll be over after I drop off twinkle toes.

Mind if I FaceTime to say Hi?

Please do.

WHILE DAD FINISHED up what looked to be a perfect rasher of bacon, I dialed Lucille's number and was delighted to see my wild-haired boy's face appear on the screen. "Hi, Mama," he shouted as he put the video to his ear.

"Hi, Love Bug. How did you sleep?"

"Good. How did you sleep?" This was our morning ritual.

"I slept well. Baba said you went swimming for a long time."

"I splashed her so big," he said with a cackle.

"I bet you did." He told me about the pool's shape and his french fries, and when he was done, I said, "I miss you, Little Man. Have fun with your daddy, okay?"

"I love you so much, Mama," he said, and then he hung up on me. And that felt perfect.

He would have a blast with his dad, as always. And I would miss him, as always. But today, I was especially glad he wasn't going to be with me. I really, really didn't want him any more involved with this mess than he already was.

Dad was just dishing out our food when Mika stumbled down. Her hair looked remarkably like Sawyer's with its wild wisps and flat side, but she seemed rested, which was good.

"You sleep okay?" I asked as she slid onto the stool next to me.

She nodded. "Is that coffee?" she asked, and Dad grabbed her a mug of her own.

"You're not vegan, right?" Dad asked.

Mika spit her coffee onto the counter. "Um, no. Bring me some of that deliciousness, please."

I smiled, happy to see her feeling spunky. It had to have been a blow to hear that her uncle may support what they were doing up at that cult compound. "So who's up for another quick episode of *Mrs. Maisel*?" I asked.

Both Dad and Mika shouted, "No, thank you," at the same time, and I cracked up.

Mika sipped her coffee and said, "I totally forgot to tell you about Marge's visit yesterday."

I snatched up a piece of bacon as soon as Dad put it in front of us and waved the half I hadn't eaten around to encourage her to get talking.

She rolled her eyes and said, "She wasn't alone. A couple of other women were with her, as usual, but there was also this dude hanging out by the door. He was clearly their escort, and from the way he kept an eye on me, I was pretty sure he'd been sent to see what they said to me."

"And?" Dad said as he handed us each a plate of cheese-filled scrambled eggs. "Did she say anything?"

"Nope, nothing beyond what was necessary to check out." Mika took a forkful of eggs and chewed while looking out the window behind Dad.

"That's the story of Marge's visit?" I said with a frown. "I thought you said she told you she was coming back in today. How did she do that if she only talked enough to buy yarn?"

Mika gave a coy shrug and shoved an entire piece of bacon in her mouth.

"You want us to guess?" I said without bothering to hide my annoyance. I had not yet had enough coffee for games. This was my one morning when I didn't have to be on the floor making truck sounds before caffeine, and I was being led into a bacon-scented round of charades.

Dad, however, seemed to enjoy the thrill of the hunt and said, "She signed it to you?"

"Nope," Mika said, "that would actually be speaking, in a sense, since American Sign Language is a language."

I rolled my eyes. This was getting more annoying by the minute.

"She had one of the other women tell you she'd be back?" Dad guessed.

"Nope," Mika said and continued to eat.

"She passed you a note," I said without a bit of enthusiasm.

Mika frowned. "You weren't supposed to guess so quickly."

I looked at her over my coffee cup and growled just a little. "What did the note say?"

"'Can't talk. I'll try to slip away tomorrow. Can I come in the back?'" Mika said, clearly peeved that I wouldn't play along.

"I assume you told her yes," Dad said.

"I did. I slipped her a note back in her change saying to ring the delivery bell at the back of the store when she arrived. Said we'd both be there." Mika sighed. "It felt a little like I was in a spy movie."

I smiled. "She's a smart one. How'd she get you the note without her handler seeing?"

"It was a green piece of paper that was cut to just the same size as her money. If she hadn't given me all ones that I had to count, I would have missed it myself." Mika smiled. "Savvy one, she is."

I finished my third piece of bacon and carried my empty plate to the dishwasher. "I better get ready then. Do you think they'll still want me for the cult if I don't shower?"

Without missing a beat, Dad said, "That may make them want you more."

I laughed all the way upstairs.

An hour later, Mika and I were at the shop, and Mika's new knitting pal, Officer Layton, was waiting at the door with a panicked look and a partially finished sweater on her hooks. Her story was that she had run out of yarn last night and needed the same dye lot to finish the baby sweater for her niece. I knew all about dye lots because I'd once started to add new stock to a partially empty bin without checking to be sure they were from the same dye lot. Mika had almost ended our friendship there and then.

Layton came in, bought two skeins of yarn, and then decided, "spur of the moment," to finish the sweater at the shop before going to the baby shower later that morning. She told us, quietly, that another officer, Spicer, would be in at eleven. Apparently, the two women knew each other from some knitting police officer's group that met in Charlottesville because Layton said, "Wait until you see the way she can turn the heel on a sock."

The level of appreciation in her voice made me actually want to see that. But mostly, I was just grateful that we were going to have police officers with us all day. We'd left Dad back at my house to do some odd jobs he'd been intending to finish anyway. It would have looked weird to have him here at the store, we knew, and besides, he would have been bored stiff all day. This way, I got new shelves in my laundry room, he got to take a nap when he wanted, and someone was keeping an eye on us while he kept an eye on my house.

I spent the morning in my usual research to learn more about the house we'd taken down the day before. I'd already done a little work at the courthouse the week before, when I'd first gotten permission to salvage, so I knew the chain of ownership of the house back to 1874 when it was built. All the owners had been local families, as best I could tell, one with twelve children living in that four-room house. I could barely survive with one in a house twice as big and couldn't imagine what that mother must have gone through.

At one point, there had been slave quarter off to the side of the house, but they had been torn down in the early twentieth century along with the kitchen and other outbuildings. The owners had sold off most of the land to a developer in the fifties, and since no one had, as best I could tell, lived in the house since the sixties, it had fallen quickly into disrepair. Someone with a lot of money could have bought it and fixed it up, but given that the lot was so small, the neighbors so close, and the damage so extensive, it had made the most sense for the owners to sell and use the lot for something else. In this case, they were going to put in a community garden for themselves and their neighbors, and I thought that a lovely idea.

Sometimes when I did this research, I found stories of inspiring people or quirky incidents – like the one house way up in the mountains that had been the site of not one but three bear attacks. Each time, the bear had died because the teenage girl who lived there was the ax-throwing champion of the county. I hadn't salvaged any bear teeth or ax heads, but that story was still one of the most popular in my newsletter.

Today, though, I was going to simply write up a general history of this house and use it as a way to talk about how houses come to be abandoned, something I'd wondered for a long time before I started this work. Turns out, most houses are abandoned because people can't agree about what to do with them. Sometimes, they're greedy about keeping the property for the sake of the earning potential, or they're so nostalgic about a place that they insist on keeping it even if they don't have the time or financial means to keep it up. Other times, wills get caught up in probate when siblings or cousins disagree about what to do with a house, and, over time, no one has the energy to keep up the fight and the house just falls into disrepair. Much more rarely, someone dies without a will. That's what I used to think happened most of the time, but alas, the tragedy isn't usually loneliness – it's greed.

I was just finishing up the draft of my main article when Lucille came in. She looked tired, more tired than even a night with a toddler might warrant, but still, she had her cake carrier. She set it down beside me in the new "cozy corner" that Mika had decided to keep even when we weren't trying to avoid prying eyes.

I was about to open the cake carrier because I knew that Lucille considered it grievously impolite to not check out her baked goods, when she practically fell into the chair beside me. I got up quickly and shouted to Mika, "Bring water and call Dad."

Lucille waved one hand. "Don't call your father, please. I'm okay. Just had a harrowing couple of blocks."

Mika had rushed over with a cup and her phone. "You sure, Lucille? You know Dad will come."

She took the ice water from Mika and sat back. "No, I'm really okay. I don't want to worry him, and besides, he needs to be at your house. Just let me sit a minute, and I'll tell you all about it."

Mika pulled a chair over and set it so that she could keep an eye on the door while she sat with us. Then, she spotted the cake carrier and said, "Is it rude if I open this?" She knew full well how Lucille liked to show off her cakes, but I appreciated her attempt at distraction.

"Please," Lucille said as she sat up a little straighter. "Just a little something I had in the freezer just in case."

Mika lifted the lid and then put her nose down to sniff. "Are those figs?"

"Quince," Lucille said as she brandished a cake knife and server from her purse. "Try some."

I stared at my stepmother and marveled at how she could foist baked goods even when she'd clearly been quite upset just moments before. But I didn't refuse a slice even in my awe, and it was delicious. Almond-flavored cake with those moist pieces of fruit. "This is so good, Lucille. But quince? Where does one buy quince? Quinces? What's the plural there?"

"I got them over at the produce market in Dayton. Picked up a case this summer and baked and baked for days. They're so delicious and underrated." Lucille served her own piece and sat back.

"It's 'quinces,'" Mika said as she slid her phone under her leg. "I had to look it up."

I ate a bite of cake, swallowed, and said, "Okay, what happened?" I was trying to be patient, and I felt sure that Lucille would have not come in with cake if Sawyer had been hurt, but the mama's heart in me was getting more and more anxious.

"First, Sawyer is fine. I dropped him off with his dad, and he went skipping to the sandbox. So don't worry." She patted my hand and then said, "Mika, do you have any coffee? I need something a bit stronger."

Mika smiled and reached for the carafe I had made and put in the work area when I sat down. "It's decaf," Mika said.

"Perfect. I just need the illusion of energy." Lucille took the mug Mika handed her. "No, this all happened after I parked up the street in the lot."

There was lots of parking street-side in our town, but a lot of people preferred to park in the little lots that dotted the businesses. It was sometimes easier to maneuver your vehicle, and you didn't have to contend with traffic when climbing in and out of the car. Lucille almost always chose a lot because she didn't like putting her baked wares at risk as she exited her car. I honestly thought that she might sacrifice her body to save a really good angel food cake. Out of respect, I would mourn her injuries while I ate that light and fluffy goodness.

"As soon as I got out of my car, two men stepped in front of me. At first, I thought they were trying to get past me to go to the ATM or something, but then when they matched my every step and wouldn't let me pass, I realized I might be in trouble."

I swallowed hard and waited for her to take another sip of coffee.

"Finally, I stopped, looked at them and said, 'What do you want?' Meanwhile, I was using my free hand to find the pepper spray in my purse. I'd never had to use it before, but I was glad I carried it all the same." She cleared her throat and said, "One of them said, 'You know Paisley Sutton?'"

I hissed. "They were looking for me?"

"Not exactly," Lucille continued. "When I told them I was your stepmother, because they obviously already knew that, they said, 'We're going to have you help her understand something, okay?'"

I winced because this felt like a scene from some mobster film, not a Saturday morning in our tiny mountain town.

"'You know, gentlemen,' I said, 'Paisley understands most things. I expect you don't need me to help you do anything.' Then I sprayed them and ran to the police station." She said that last part so casually that she might have been talking about trying on a pair of sneakers at the mall.

"You pepper sprayed them? Really!?" Mika clapped with delight. "You are my new hero."

I stared at my stepmom and then started a slow clap as I stood to hug her. She blushed as I bent down to grab her neck, but the smile on her face also told me she appreciated the enthusiastic reaction.

"The police arrested them?" Mika asked.

"I'm not sure they were formally arrested, but the deputy in charge, an attractive young man who was knitting when I came in, went right out, cuffed them, and brought them into the station while Officer Winslow took my statement." She studied her hands. "They didn't look happy though. I hope I didn't make it worse."

I sighed. "I don't think you could make it worse," I said, "But Officer Layton up there might know something." I glanced over at Mika, and she was already on the move. It just made the most sense for the store owner to talk to a customer, and while I was sure whoever was watching us knew I was in here, too, I didn't need to draw attention to myself by sitting in the front window and talking about something I knew nothing about.

"Are you okay though?" I asked as I studied Lucille's face.

She nodded. "I am . . . although I will say that I haven't really been that frightened in a long time. Jerks!" Lucille definitely used more colorful language than that regularly, but she was respecting Mika's business, I expected.

We sat in the quiet for a few minutes until Mika came back. "Layton checked in. Your boys were released since they hadn't actually committed a formal crime, but they are being watched closely. Santiago is on his way, too. He's not liking the sound of this stuff, Layton said."

I stood up and stretched. So much for finishing my newsletter today. I couldn't concentrate if I wanted to. "I'm going to start organizing early. I need to keep busy."

"Want some help?" Lucille said. "I thought I might go over to your place later, see if I could get your dad to watch something and relax for a couple of hours. But right now, I just want to stay put and do something with my hands. You mind?" She looked from me to Mika.

Mika said, "No, please help. Paisley can show you her system."

I put my arm through my stepmother's and led her to the back room. "First, we need to pick our shelf enhancers."

"You read too much Ellery Adams," she said with a smile.

"If you know the term, then I could say the same about you." I laughed and pointed toward the shelves where I kept the odds and ends I picked up on my salvage jobs. Today, Lucille chose a beautiful brass sconce that had lost its mate, an old-fashioned house number sign that read 313, and a shoe rack Dad had cobbled together from reclaimed baseboards. The back doorbell rang as we gathered our items and took stock of the yarn inventory, and I saw Mika pass by the storeroom on her way to answer it.

As Lucille and I walked back out to the main floor, our arms full of knickknacks, I saw Mika talking in the cozy corner with a young woman in very simple clothes – a long skirt and tennis shoes beneath her pilled blue sweater. That had to be Marge.

Mika caught my eye, but she quickly turned her attention back to the woman. I took the hint and kept on with the organizing. We started at the front of the store this time and took note of what needed restocking, what was sold out, and where we had room to put the new items Mika had added to her inventory. Business had been pretty good lately, so Mika was increasing her offerings a bit.

As I stalked back and forth to the storeroom for skeins of yarn, I did my best to ignore Mika and the woman, even though I was dying to eavesdrop. But I knew that if I showed too much interest, the woman might bolt, or worse, the spies in the brown pickup that was, again, parked out front might wonder what I was doing. So Lucille and I kept at it.

I spent a lot of time in the alpaca section organizing but also caressing the skeins. I hadn't said anything to Sawyer because time was a concept that only included "now" for him, but when he started school, I was thinking I might get two alpacas and a miniature donkey. I'd been looking at the listings for fiber animals that were retiring, and I thought in a couple of years, I could save up the cash and enjoy the animals while also giving Mika the fiber. The miniature donkey was just because they were so cute, but I'd tell Dad it was because they were good guard animals.

Lucille had a knack for display, so she was moving the shelf enhancers around the store as I reorganized the yarn. She put the shoe rack on a lower shelf of big, bulky one-pound skeins of yarn and then artfully tucked some of the most vibrant colors in the cubbies. It was a great use of the shelf and showed an option for how a customer might use it. I predicted the shelf would be sold within a week.

As the two of us moved around the room and got closer to where Mika and Marge were talking, I struck up a casual baking conversation with Lucille by asking about her favorite kind of scones. She took up the conversational cause without pause and starting telling me about using figs and pears in scones as well as the merits of clotted cream versus whipped cream. Soon, we had made our way into the nook where Mika and Marge were talking.

I was just beginning to admire the chunky variegated yarns that Mika kept mid-store for, as she said, the serious afghan makers, when Marge stood up and hugged Mika quickly before moving along the side of the store so that she could slip out the back door again. She had been smart in her movements, and I doubted that anyone outside had been able to see her.

Officer Layton casually stood as Marge made it to the back and headed that way herself, leaving her yarn on the chair. She feigned going into the bathroom just for show and then darted down the hall to the back door. Mika walked up beside me. "She's going to be sure Marge gets to her car okay. Just in case."

I nodded. "Good idea. Help us refill the Lion Brand bins and give us the scoop?"

A quick scan of the store told Mika no one else was inside, and she and I joined Lucille where she was elbow deep in a rust-colored yarn. "This color looks like a sunset," she said.

I ran my hands over a few skeins and thought of my mom, who had helped me paint a wall in my first house this exact color a few years back. Goodness, I missed her. "Maybe someday I'll crochet a blanket in this shade," I said and wished, for the forty-millionth time, that she was here for me to talk to her.

Mika squeezed my arm and then began to group the small sets of yarn into a miscellaneous bin and said, "Marge told me just what we need to do tomorrow."

For the next hour, Lucille, Mika, and I sketched out a plan based on Marge's guidance. She had been immensely helpful, despite being, as Mika put it, "as terrified as a mouse caught in a closet with a cat."

We were just putting the final touches on our strategy for the morning worship service when Santiago came in with Mary Johnson. I hadn't seen Mary since the visit to Olivia's house, and I was happy to see her in her own right. But I was also eager to hear how Olivia was. Mary hadn't been my friend for that long, but weekly meals after Sunday church and long afternoons of playing cards had given us a chance to know each other well rather quickly. She was a good person, and I was glad to see her.

I was more glad to see the sheriff than I probably should have been. Still, his gentle touch on my hand as he sat down in the wingback chair next to me was a welcome bit of warmth on what already felt like a very long day.

The five of us squeezed into the semi-hidden nook with

Mika's chair, again, edged out so she could keep an eye on the door. Her position wasn't really necessary since Officer Dutch, Layton's relief, was perusing the yarn very carefully. She was, apparently, a big crocheter of prayer shawls in her spare time, and she was eager to crochet while on duty. According to Santiago, she was also a great police officer, the best from Orange, he said. She may have been browsing, but she also had a sharp eye out for anything, including customers.

Still, I understood Mika's vigilance. I was aching to get back to my newsletter. There was just something about running a business for yourself that made it especially hard to put down, even when you needed to give it a rest sometimes.

We caught Santiago up on Marge's advice, and he nodded grimly. "Okay, that sounds like a feasible plan to get you back to the compound, but we also need to build in some fail-safes just in case."

"You want me to wear a wire?" Mika asked with so much enthusiasm that I knew we had to stop watching police dramas for a while.

"No, Officer Dutch will be wearing the mic," Santiago said firmly. "She's already attended the church twice, and no one will be watching her particularly closely."

I looked again at the woman shopping the super-heavy-weight yarn. She was about sixty, I guessed, with a cute bob to her silver hair and sensible Merrell shoes on her feet. In other words, she was not what I imagined when I thought of an undercover police officer, but then, maybe that was the point.

Mika seemed quite disappointed that she wasn't going to get a button cam or some such, but she did like what Santiago had to say next. "If you need help, though, and you can't get Officer Dutch's attention, you need to just get to the light switch and flip the lights on and off a couple of times. If we see that, we'll come right in."

"Flick the lights three times. Got it," Mika said, like she was taking notes for undercover class.

"No, not three times. Just once. Just lean against the switch like it's an accident. It's going to take us a minute to get there, and you can play off the mistake with one flicker. But not three." He gave Mika a stern look before continuing. When it seemed she got the point, he said, "Officer Dutch has also already secured an invitation to lunch tomorrow, so you'll have eyes and ears there, too. But we won't be as close. So you need to try and stay near her, okay?"

"How do we do that?" I asked.

"By making friends with me now," Officer Dutch said from just on the other side of the bins of yarn behind me. "We'll spend some time together today, and then tomorrow, you can be delighted to see me at church, okay?"

I smiled. "Sounds like a plan. Maybe in a few minutes you can teach me to crochet?" I actually did want to learn to do more than I could, but more, my entrepreneur's heart was aching to get back to my email. Still, this part of the charade took precedence because I wanted this all done and settled before Sawyer came over tomorrow.

"Okay, then," Santiago said as he stood up. "Now, we need to just sell my visit, so Mika, will you come outside with me to talk about how Paisley is doing and your concerns about her father?"

Lucille rolled her eyes. "And that's my signal to go. I don't think you can pull off that BS with his wife nearby." She bent over and kissed my cheek. "Thanks for letting me stick around and help. See you at your place later?"

"Yep," I said as I stood up to stretch and casually greet Officer Dutch while Mika and Santiago went to do their performance on the sidewalk out front and keep an eye on Lucille while she went to her car. She texted when she was safely on the road. *No incidents*, her message said.

I poured Mary a glass of wine from Mika's stash and sat with her behind the screen of yarn for a few minutes. "I'm sorry I won't be at our church tomorrow. I'll miss lunch, too. What are you all playing tomorrow?"

"Tomorrow is Spoons, so you may be glad to miss it. Bertha can get downright brutal in her spoon-grabbing," Mary said with a laugh. "But seriously, Paisley, are you sure you want to do this? I mean these people are pretty awful, and while Olivia will appreciate what you're doing, it's not going to bring Stephen back."

I sighed. "I know. I just can't let those women suffer without doing everything I can, and if it helps to bring justice for Rocket, too . . . I mean, what if something I find out tomorrow implicates Scott?"

"And what if it doesn't? We don't know that he did this, Paisley." Mary sipped her wine and held my gaze.

"I know. But he seems the most likely suspect, right?" The man clearly had issues with women, and maybe Rocket Sutherland had gotten in his way.

"He does, but I do need to tell you something else. Something that Olivia probably didn't say."

I tilted my head and leaned forward. "What is it? Did Rocket have some secret life we don't know about yet?"

"Not Rocket," she said quietly. "Renee."

I sat up straight. "What? What do you mean?"

"Olivia doesn't like to talk ill about anyone, and Renee has been through a lot. But she's also made some really bad choices, choices that had big consequences." Mary's voice was kind but clear.

I studied her face a moment and said, "You mean Nadia?" I scowled. "You're not implying that because she had a child without being married that she's some sort of awful person, are you, Mary?"

Mary shook her head. "No, not at all. Of course not. What I

am saying is that Nadia's father was another member of Mountain Green, and Nadia was not a planned pregnancy."

I took a deep breath. "Mary, please just be straight with me here. All this coded talk—"

Mary interrupted. "You're right. Sorry. Olivia has been protecting Renee and Nadia for so long that I think it wore off on me." She looked up at the ceiling and then met my gaze again. "Nadia is a product of a 'non-consensual relationship,' – her term, not mine - at Mountain Green."

I dropped back in my chair. "Oh my goodness, Mary. Poor Renee. But you said she made a poor choice. I thought you were implying that her choice to have sex was poor."

"No, her choice to join that group of woman-haters. That's what I was talking about." She shook her head. "Sorry, that sounds like I'm blaming her. I'm not. But I wish someone had been able to convince her to stay away. After Rocket died, though, she was just not herself."

I took the ponytail holder out of my hair and ran my fingers against my scalp to think. "They were really in love, then, huh?"

Mary frowned and looked away for a minute. "That's what most people think."

"But you don't?" I asked as I sat forward again.

"I think Rocket loved Renee. I think he would have done anything for her, but it always seemed to me that Renee was a little too into Rocket, if you know what I mean?"

"You think she was using him?" I asked.

Mary shrugged. "I'm not sure, but I thought you should know that Renee has connections up in the Hollow, too. Might make a difference tomorrow when you go up there."

I nodded and hugged her as she stood to leave. "Thanks, Mary. I'll let you know how it goes?"

"Please do," she said and then grabbed a piece of Lucille's quince cake for the road. "Get me this recipe?"

"Sure thing," I said.

I didn't have much time to think about what Mary had told me because I needed to build my cover for tomorrow. I headed to the front of the store, where Officer Dutch was pretending to puzzle over yarn choices, and introduced myself.

Officer Dutch, or Lindy, as she said to call her, was actually a stellar undercover shopper and a great crochet teacher. We spent two hours together that afternoon, and between learning about her deep love of Irish Wolfhounds – she had two, Finneus and Lucretia – and getting her impressions of the Mountain Green men, who she characterized as men with ideas of women that belonged in the Middle Ages, she actually taught me a very basic but entirely lovely shell stitch that didn't require me to count and helped me create the beginnings of a queen-sized afghan for my own bed. It was a lovely way to spend the day.

About four, she headed out, and I saw a cruiser pull up out front. Officer Winslow went into the coffee shop across the way, and a few moments later, I noticed her sitting at a table by the window sipping a huge mug of something. Our protection still in place, I took out my laptop, posted my latest offerings on the auction site I used, and finished off both my newsletter and the links to my listings. Once I had the article scheduled to send, I just had to hope someone was looking for a couple dozen crystal door knobs and a vintage phone nook. They were the small things I'd been able to salvage from the house yesterday, and until I could get the mantels and other bigger pieces like doors cleaned up, these bits and bobs were all I had to bring me some income.

With my work done and about twenty minutes left until Mika closed, I finished organizing the shelves and gathering up the skeins of yarn I needed to finish my own afghan. While I stacked and shopped, I thought about Stephen Sutherland and wondered if all this sleuthing about Mountain Green was going to get us any information about his death. I was quite happy to hopefully expose the harmful treatment of women there, but I'd gotten into this thing because that poor young man had died. And now, I had found out that his girlfriend had ties to the church that might just make this all the more complicated.

It was going to be a doozy of a dinnertime conversation at my house that night.

11

When Mika and I got back to my place, Dad had the Weber grill going by the front porch, and I could smell beef sizzling. Dad was making steak, and I was here for it. I didn't grill out much myself, mostly because the process involved to get the charcoal going and super-hot was often impossible with a toddler around. Either I was interrupted a hundred times, or he was bound and determined to burn all the flesh off his arms by reaching into the coals. I could have gotten a gas grill, I knew, but it just wasn't worth it, especially if the odds were good that Sawyer wouldn't eat whatever I took the time to grill anyway. Better to stick with hot dogs, chicken nuggets, and Paw Patrol waffles for the next couple of years. Most days, I was just glad he really liked fruit.

Inside my kitchen, Lucille was pulling baked potatoes out of my oven, and I could see green beans steaming on the range. This was going to be a great dinner . . . a nice counter to all the drama we were living through. My stepmother saw us, assessed our stress levels, and pulled out the Kahlua and milk. It was a White Russian kind of night, and she knew it.

With our drinks poured, Mika and I set the table. My place

settings were nothing fancy – purple and orange placemats, the pottery-like dishes I'd gotten a couple of decades earlier, and the blue-rimmed glasses that Mom and I found in a really sketchy thrift store across from the gas station that my high school friends and I had called the "drug and gas" since everyone knew it was the place to buy anything illicit. And trust me, if I, Miss Twentieth Century Pollyanna, knew you could get drugs there, everyone knew.

Dad brought in the steaks, and my mouth began to water. I so rarely ate really good food, let alone food I didn't have to cook, that I felt like crying when Lucille also set out a beautiful Caesar salad with *lots* of croutons. Dad said a blessing for our meal, and then we all tucked in, eager to eat – and, if everyone else felt like I did, to also put off the conversation for just a bit longer.

It couldn't wait forever, though, so once I had a few bites of everything in me, I told them what Mary had said about Renee. "I don't really know what to make of that. Mary would never tell me something like that to disparage Renee or Nadia. I think she really wanted me to see the whole picture of things."

Mika frowned. "I don't know Mary as well as you, but I do like her. Still, I don't like it when women talk about other women in ways that imply the things people have done to them are their own fault."

Dad cleared his throat. "I'm just a guy here, so I'm probably going to get this really wrong, but it sounds to me like Mary is just saying that Renee made a bad choice about the company she kept, not that this choice justified anything after that."

I smiled, and Lucille spoke with pride before I could. "That was well said, Baby. That's my take, too, but I'm like you, Mika, there's too much conversation about what women should do differently and not near enough about what men need to change."

"I guess," I said, "the reasons behind Mary telling me don't matter as much as what she told me. I know she wasn't lying, so I guess the question is why Renee didn't tell us. After all, she pretty much blamed Mountain Green for Scott's behavior, but she totally neglected to mention that she was involved with the church, too. That feels off to me."

Mika nodded. "Me, too. Feels like she's hiding something."

"She may be," Lucille said. "The question is what? Is it that she's embarrassed to have ever been involved with them? Misplaced shame from the rape? Or something more? Something that might be connected to Rocket Sutherland's death?"

We all ate in silence for a bit until Dad said, "I'm going up to the Hollow tomorrow." He said it in the same tone of voice that he might announce he was headed to bed: matter-of-fact and indisputable.

I sighed. I had long ago learned it did no good to argue with my father, but Lucille was newer and better at this than I was. She was also not his daughter, so she said, "Why in the world would you do that?"

"My baby girl is going up that mountain, and so am I." He pushed back from the table and began to clear the dishes. "Who wants ice cream with their apple pie?"

This part of the conversation was clearly over for now, but the shake of Lucille's head told me that it wasn't over for her. I wished her a silent bit of luck.

After dinner, we all cleaned up the table and then began a near-epic battle of gin rummy. My dad was not a game player, but even he got into the spirit. We played for two hours, and the smack-talk was golden. My stepmother called my father "a good-for-nothing fool," to which he responded by picking up the entire discard deck and then going out with something like eighty billion points. In the next hand, Mika told Lucille that she was about to go down like cake without a rising agent. To anyone else, that would have been a lame insult, but to Lucille, those were fighting words. You didn't impugn her baking or her card playing, and she dominated the next three hands.

I held my own with my usual foolhardy desire to pick up as many cards as I could possibly use, and one hand out of three I won. In the end, though, Dad was the champion, and he gloated by eating another small piece of apple pie. The events of the past few days had left us all exhausted, so at nine p.m., we began to put up and lock up. We checked the doors, and Dad checked the windows again. I let Beauregard out for his usual constitutional because, in this way alone, he thought he was a dog. And just as he was coming back inside, a vehicle pulled down the farm lane.

I literally ran back inside, shooing Beau ahead of me, and screamed, "Daddy!" The terror in my voice scared me further, but I had recognized that pickup truck.

My dad came from the back of the house, shotgun in hand, and I just pointed out the front window. Dad looked out quickly and said, "He's coming to the door. If I greet him this way, your plan for tomorrow is shot."

I sighed and looked at Mika. She looked terrified, but she nodded, and Dad quickly tucked himself into the pantry at the back of the kitchen. Lucille turned back to the sink and resumed washing dishes like nothing major was going on.

A few seconds later, Nick Sterit knocked on my door. It would have been dumb to act like I hadn't seen him coming because he had to have seen me running, cat at my feet, into the house, so instead, I peeked around the edge of the door's window like I was scared to see who was there. Then, when I was sure he had seen me see him, I grabbed Mika's hand and pulled her to the door. We opened the door, hand-in-hand, and the look of terror on our faces was, I'm sure, convincing because it was genuine.

Nick smiled in a winsome way that, without any backstory,

might have been charming but now just set my skin crawling. "Evening, ladies. Sorry to come so late. I think I might have scared you."

I waited a beat, thinking he might apologize or say something about not intending to terrify, but he didn't. So I said, "It's okay. Can we help you?"

He looked from Mika to me and then over at Lucille behind us. "Your father isn't here anymore?"

I clenched my jaw so as not to hiss at his audacity. "He's already gone to bed," I said. "Daddy needs his rest."

Behind me, I heard Lucille drop a mug in the sink, but I didn't turn around. Santa Man didn't seem to notice. "I see," he said. "Well, just wanted to be sure you ladies were still planning on coming to church in the morning."

"Yes, sir, we are," Mika said quietly. "We're looking forward to it."

"Good, good. Just wanted to be sure Marge hadn't scared you off." He stood silently, waiting.

"Marge? No, she's the one who told us to come visit, remember?" Mika said, her voice tight.

"Well, two visits in two days got us worried that she might be overselling a little bit, I guess." Nick waited a beat, just to let that sink in. "But I'm glad to see you're still interested."

"Definitely," I said. Then, I decided to go for broke. "I'd invite you in, Mr. Sterit, but it's getting late, and since Daddy is in bed, it wouldn't really be appropriate—"

Santa Man cut me off. "No, no it wouldn't. I'm glad you know that. We all know us men can be scoundrels. Wouldn't want you all to be stumbling blocks for me, now would we?" His tone was so condescending that it made my teeth hurt. "I'll just see you both in the morning. You, too, if you want to come, Mrs. Sutton."

"No, thank you, sir. And it's Ms. Nundrum." The edge to her voice was razor-sharp.

Nick rolled his eyes and said, "Good night, ladies."

I resisted the urge to slam the door behind him and closed it gently. Then, Lucille stopped fake-washing the last mug, Dad stepped out of the dark pantry with his shotgun still at the ready, and I turned off the lights in the kitchen. We made our way into the living room, the only room where all the windows could be blocked, and sat down.

"What an ass," my dad said. My dad *never* swore, so this was a huge moment . . . and I appreciated it because I was scared out of my mind.

"That was clearly intimidation," Mika said.

"You think?" I snapped, and then immediately regretted the way my fear had taken over my tongue when I saw the hurt on Mika's face. "I'm sorry. I'm just scared. He didn't even try to explain how he knew where I lived or act surprised that you were here."

"They're shameless," Lucille said. "People who act that way wouldn't hesitate to kill someone and bury their body."

I sighed because I knew she was right. It's possible that Rocket Sutherland's killer had just stood on my front porch. The thought chilled me to my bones.

"You still going to try to talk me out of going up there with them tomorrow?" Dad asked Lucille.

"Nope, and I'm going too. Do you have another one of those?" She pointed to the gun lying across Dad's knees.

"You tell me where to shoot, and I'll do the dirty work," he said with exhausted humor. "I do think we all need to go to bed. The house is secure, and I'm taking Old Bart up there with me."

"Your gun has a name?" I said.

"It does now." Dad stood and headed up the stairs, Bart over his shoulder.

We all trudged up without even thinking about brushing our teeth or using the bathroom. Bed and comfort just sounded too tempting.

I'd tried to convince Dad and Lucille to take my bed and let Mika and me share Sawyer's, but they had refused. And I was actually grateful. The comfort of my own divot in the mattress was not something I wanted to give up tonight, especially if I couldn't sleep.

Mika and I got into our pajamas and then climbed into bed. I could feel the tears creeping up my throat, so I turned to her and said, "You think Sawyer's okay, right?"

She took my hand. "I do. I don't think they're interested in hurting anyone, and if they can recruit you, then they'll get him, too. So there's no reason to be bothering with him."

I swallowed hard and tried to stop crying. "Is it weird if I text his dad?"

"Not weird at all. Go ahead." She picked up her e-reader.

Sawyer do okay today? Just checking in since he had an unusual night last night.

Doing great. Ate well. Good nap. Went to sleep no problem. He said he had fun with Lucille.

Okay, good. Thanks. Hug him for me?

Sure.

When I put my phone down, Mika laid her e-reader on her chest. "He okay?"

"Yep, just fine. Nothing out of the ordinary." I sighed. "I know his dad would tell me if something weird was going on."

I looked over at my best friend. "You still want to do this?" I asked her as I got out my own e-reader, already loaded with the latest Ellery Adams book. "We don't have to go tomorrow."

"We are going. We have a plan. We need answers about Rocket and information about what's happening to the women up there." She got quiet for a minute. "And I really need to see if Marge is okay."

I had totally forgotten about Marge. The Mountain Green

men were clearly suspicious of her. "I should tell Santiago about that."

"Good plan." She picked up her book again and rolled away from me as if I needed privacy to text.

They know Marge was in again today. Sterit stopped by my house.

We saw him come up and over the railroad tracks. I came over right away, but since he was gone but probably still watching, I didn't stop. There's an unmarked car with Officer Layton on duty at the cabinet shop across the tracks.

Okay. Thanks. And Marge?

We will try to pick her up tomorrow when we get you two out. See if we can help her find a new place.

Okay. Going to try to get some sleep now.

Good plan. Wish I could be there to sit with you until you do. Night.

Night.

I STARED at my phone for a few moments before turning on the sound and setting it on my bedside table. Most of the time, I kept the sound off because the vibration was enough to tell me I had a message. But tonight, I wanted to be sure to wake up if someone tried to reach me for any reason. And I really wished Santiago was here, too, for comfort and peace of mind.

Fortunately, I didn't have any trouble falling asleep, and I got in a few good hours before I had to pee. But once I had made it downstairs, done what I needed to do, and climbed back into bed, my brain was racing. I lay there for a bit, but when fifteen minutes had passed and four a.m. had come, I decided to just get up. I slipped downstairs again and grabbed my sewing basket and a quilt to put on my lap. Then, I sat on the couch and began to sew.

I was stitching in the shadowed side of the barn, and most

of the stiches were black. So as long as I counted well, I made quick progress. I loved stitching complicated patterns with blended floss and lots of color variation, but tonight, I needed to see the lines of *x*'s march across the fabric in quick succession. Soon, I had that side of the barn stitched, and I got to move on to more of the whites of the snow beyond. By the time the sun came up a couple hours later, I had put in a few hundred stitches, more than I'd done in the past month. I held the work up to the light and then stood to stretch, my mind relaxed, if completely exhausted.

Still, sewing always calmed me, and I knew it was better to go into the morning with a little less sleep but more clarity of spirit. I packed up my basket and stowed it away again so Saw couldn't give his stuffed bear another haircut with my sewing scissors while I was in the shower. Then, I headed to the kitchen, found my insulated coffee carafe, and got the French press going. We were all going to need a lot of caffeine.

Coffee brewing, I pulled out the brand-new pound of thick-cut bacon I'd taken out of the freezer the night before and kicked up the griddle. Next, I measured out the steel-cut oatmeal and water and got that boiling. We all needed hearty fortification, and I needed to stay busy.

While the food cooked, I tidied up the house and set the table. Typically, breakfast was a process of me fixing plates and setting them out, but, today, I thought we'd be a little more do-it-yourself. I put a bowl of raisins out first and filled the antique creamer-and-sugar set that a dear friend had gifted me when I moved into the farmhouse. Then, I set out four mugs with matching plates and bowls and prepped a platter with paper towels for the bacon. Last but not least, I set out the silverware as Mom had taught me and even slipped a paper napkin under each fork.

Just as I was flipping the bacon, Mika wandered into the kitchen. She was wearing a long, pleated wool skirt over purple leggings, a black sweater with what I thought was an oxford-cloth shirt underneath, and absolutely no jewelry or makeup. She looked like a mourning doll, but without the lace. "Well, you look the part," I said.

She smiled. "The purple leggings don't ruin it? I just get so cold in skirts, and I didn't have anything else that wasn't, well, fishnet."

"Actually, I think it works. It's 'modest'"—I made air quotes because I hated that word—"because your skin is covered, but it's also so mismatched that it'll probably give the impression that you're frugal or poor, both of which are qualities I think the Mountain Green folks will find appealing."

"Oh, good, I look poor and frumpy. Good. Good," she said.

"Unfortunately, I think that's our aesthetic for the day. Mind keeping an eye on things while I go put on my own surfeit of clothing?"

She slid into my spot by the stove and stirred the oatmeal as I jogged upstairs to dress before the food was finished cooking. I had decided on a deep purple skirt that I'd bought a few years earlier in Harpers Ferry. It was flowing and hung to my ankles, and normally, I wore it in summer with sandals and a tank top. Today, though, I was putting on the most old-fashioned shoes I owned – black Mary Jane clogs – and tights. On top, I donned a simple, long-sleeved T-shirt and one of Mom's old black cardigans. It tied at the waist, and normally, I wouldn't have left the house in it because it made me look like I had two inches of torso. Today, though, it was perfect.

I pulled my hair into a tight ponytail and opted for the one actual headband I owned to hold the wispy pieces out of my face. Normally, I rolled up a bandana and tied it on, but I thought that might look a little too, well, I didn't know what, so the headband that I'd had since fifth grade, literally, would do the trick.

As I came out of my room, Dad and Lucille emerged from

Sawyer's room, and they looked like they'd just walked out of the woods. Both of them were in head-to-toe camo, and Lucille even had paint on her face. Dad's gun was over his shoulder, and Lucille was carrying what looked like a billy club. I cracked up, which was not the reaction they were hoping for, I gathered.

"Why are you laughing? We're going to protect you, Baby Girl," Dad said with a frown.

I tried to stop laughing, but the two of them looked ridiculous. I pointed down the stairs when I couldn't get my giggles under control enough to say, "Breakfast."

As they followed me down the stairs, I heard Lucille say, "As if she didn't look like the wayward cousin from *Witness* herself."

I kept laughing because, well, she wasn't wrong.

In the kitchen, Mika was just setting the platter of bacon on the table when we walked in. She looked at me and then at Dad and Lucille and said, "Casting for that new reality show where people try to live as pioneers isn't until next week, y'all." Then she doubled over in laughter.

"Look who's talking, Ma Clampett," Dad said . . . And then he broke into a grin, and we all sat down with laughter filling the air.

"You packed all that stuff two days ago?" I asked as I loaded my oatmeal with raisins and brown sugar.

"Be prepared," Dad said.

"You can take the boy out of the Boy Scouts . . ." Lucille said with a smile.

The levity faded quickly, though, as the danger and stakes of what we were about to do settled in. Today, we would either find out who Rocket's killer was and give Santiago enough to at least investigate the church for assaults on women, or we would become victims ourselves. It didn't seem like there was much in between those two options. It was all or nothing.

We ate and cleaned up in silence, and when it was time to

go, Dad and Lucille gave us quick hugs and then disappeared into the laundry room to wait away from prying eyes while Mika and I opened up the blinds and headed out. The church wasn't far away, but Marge had said it would be good if we came early, to show how eager we were to be there. So at ten a.m., we pulled out of my driveway, and I said a silent prayer for help for all of us.

Dad and Lucille were going to head out in a few minutes with the hopes that whoever was watching us would move along when we did. Then, they were going to set up in the woods behind the church after driving up to the winery via the other side of the mountain. Santiago wasn't thrilled with that idea because it made him responsible for more people, but he couldn't really stop them, not after the winery owner gave his enthusiastic permission for them to use his land. He wanted Mountain Green shut down as much as anybody because he'd heard about what was happening with women there, too . . . and because the church members harassed him about selling the "devil's drink."

Santiago and his team were going to be at the boarding school just down the Hollow, and another team was staging at the gas station at the bottom of the mountain. Everyone would be in plain clothes and as out of sight as possible, and, if we gave the signal, they'd be in that church in no time flat. The key was that we be able to give the signal, and the closer we got to the church, the less confident I felt about that possibility. Something in me was saying we'd been made, and I couldn't shake that feeling.

Plus, if I was honest, I wasn't too keen on sitting through this whole church service. My church was a lively place with lots of conversation and great music, and the pastor spoke with fire and fervor about justice and compassion. I did not think that was what I was going to find here, and the idea of sitting through a sermon where women might be denigrated . . . well, I was already grinding my teeth as we pulled up.

My anxiety had me wanting to bounce around and talk to everyone, but I reined myself in, took a deep breath, and tried to look small and scared. The scared part wasn't hard, but no one had ever said I had a small personality. So I decided to not even try to curb my bad habit of biting my fingernails. It would keep me busy and be in character for sure.

When we arrived, we weren't the first ones there, but all the other congregation members were already seated in their pews with their heads bowed. A stern man with lamb-chop sideburns handed us a printed bulletin and said, dourly, "Welcome." Mika and I said quiet thank-yous and then headed to the far side of the church to sit.

Given that we were quite early, I had a lot of time to inspect the building. It was beautiful in a very simple way. A wooden cross hung at the front, and the translucent windows along the sides of the sanctuary let in the bright morning sun. The carpet was burgundy, and the pews an orangey pine. The place itself was lovely, but the atmosphere was so heavy, so solemn that I was having trouble getting my breath.

I loved a reverent space where people were steeped in prayer and contemplation. I had once spent two hours in Canterbury Cathedral just watching people light candles and say prayers. It was beautiful. This place, though, didn't have that open, hopeful feel. Here, I just felt weighed down, overburdened. Once again, I wished I was at my church, where everyone would be talking, and the organist would be playing, and someone would surely laugh.

Mika and I exchanged a few glances, and then finally she leaned over and whispered right in my ear. "I don't like it here."

I nodded and mouthed, "Me neither," and continued to watch people file in. The men were all in suits and the women all in long dresses or skirts; even the children were formal. And everyone was white, another thing that was very different from my church, where most of the congregation was black.

I saw Lindy slide into place a couple of pews ahead of us and felt just a bit of my anxiety lessen.

A few minutes before eleven, the organist sat down and began to play a hymn I loved, "O for a Thousand Tongues to Sing." Normally, this was an up-tempo number where people could blast out praise of God, but here, it felt like a funeral dirge. The pace was slow, and the notes too bloated to feel joyful. I couldn't *wait* to hear the singing.

The only real solace in the service was that it followed the traditional order I knew from the churches of my childhood. Welcome and announcements. A hymn. Scripture reading and prayers. Another hymn, followed by the sermon, and another hymn to close the hour. I leaned into that familiarity when the singing started because even though we sang "Crown Him with Many Crowns" and "Amazing Grace," I just didn't feel the hope or joy I usually felt when a group of people gathered to focus on something other than strife or difference. Instead, when the service ended, I felt sad and kind of alone. I held onto Mika's hand tightly because I needed to be reminded I had friends . . . and because we were about to do the hard part.

Marge's suggested plan hinged on one thing – that we get Reverend Villay to invite us to lunch at the compound. Apparently, if this invitation was extended, then we could consider ourselves as good as accepted. Our acting skills and our backstories were about to come into play during this short fellowship time at the back of the sanctuary.

Mika and I headed toward the folding tables that had been set up in the vestibule. Big silver percolators of coffee sat next to paper plates filled with sandwich cookies and gingersnaps. This, too, felt familiar, and for a moment, I felt a bit more at ease.

But then I saw Renee, Scott, and Nadia, and all the air left my lungs. They must have come in after the service started, and I'd been too nervous to try and look around much. So their presence was a complete surprise, and given that Mika was about to break the fingers in my hand, I gathered it was a surprise to her, too. Even with what Mary had told us, I still couldn't believe she was there, and with her brother, too.

It didn't look like she'd noticed us yet, so I dragged Mika toward a group of women and slid behind them, hoping to stay unnoticed. Once it was time for lunch, we might have a few minutes before heading up the mountain to strategize with Santiago.

Fortunately, Marge was in the small circle of women I'd pulled us toward, and Mika said, "Hi, Marge," with genuine warmth.

Marge looked at her and smiled before introducing us to the women she was with. Then, she took my hand and held it before her, saying, "So very glad you could join us, Paisley." She smiled again before letting go of my hand.

As she did, I felt the note against my palm and looked up to see the panic in Marge's eyes. I smiled and nodded as if acknowledging her welcome even as my brain raced to try and figure out exactly how I was going to read this note.

I was just trying to scheme a way to turn my back for a moment when Mika leaned forward into the circle and said, "Is there a bathroom I can use? Too much tea this morning." She giggled a little, and I really had to work hard not to snort at her overacting.

It worked, though, because one of the women pointed to a small door at the side of the room. "Thank you," Mika said. "We'll be right back." Then she pulled me quickly behind her. The stereotype about women going to the bathroom together was working in our favor because no one paid us any mind. I was glad that they had indeed added indoor bathrooms as I didn't think two women could go into an outhouse as easily.

As soon as we were in the door and had checked to be sure we were alone, I said, "Did you see Marge pass me the note?"

"Note?! What note?"

I was confused. "Wait, why did you ask for us to go to bathroom if you didn't see the note?"

"What note?" Mika asked, her frustration rising as she kept an eye on the door.

"This note." I held it up. "Marge passed it to me." I began to unfold it.

"I didn't know about the note, but Renee was headed toward us. We've been spotted." She stared at the door as if she knew what was going to come.

"Oh no." I shoved the note into Mika's hand and then pushed her into one of the two powder-pink stalls just as the door to the bathroom opened.

"Paisley, what a surprise to see you," Renee said. Her smile was frigid, and I felt a shiver go down my spine.

Behind me, I heard the toilet flush, and Mika stepped out and put on the best performance of her life. If I hadn't known better, even I would have thought she was surprised. Her eyes went wide, and her hands flew up by her face as she said, "Renee, oh my goodness. What a surprise." She washed her hands quickly and then stepped forward and took Renee's hands as she said, "Are you okay? Why are you here?" Her voice even got quieter as she asked.

For a moment, Renee's face stayed hard, but then, she seemed to change her mind about something and said, "Oh, I'm okay. Just missed my family, that's all."

Then, she looked at me and said, "Scott said he was sorry, and he bought me flowers. I thought I owed him another chance."

I stared at her for a moment as my brain spun and I tried to decide the best course of action. I concluded that honesty would read best in the moment. "Renee, you know that men often apologize and don't really mean it, right?"

Renee smiled and said, "He does mean it, though, and he says we can come up here and live with Reverend Villay. That means Nadia will have friends and be around all these great people. It'll be so nice to have a real community, you know?"

I wasn't buying this nonsense for a second, but I was wise enough to know that now wasn't the time to let her know I was onto her. I swallowed and said, "Okay, but if you need us, you know where to find us."

Mika stepped back beside me. "Actually, we were hoping to, well, maybe, move up here, too. Being a part of a community just sounds so nice."

Gracious, Mika was good. Her voice had just the right amount of pitifulness to be believable. "Yeah, I'm still not sure, but if Mika thinks it's a good idea, I trust her." I hoped Mika was getting my message to tread carefully.

Mika took my hand and squeezed a piece of paper into my palm. "Your turn," she said as she pointed toward the stall behind me.

I took my cue and slipped inside. I even made myself pee for the sake of credibility while Mika made small talk about Nadia with Renee. When I opened the folded offering envelope, I saw that Marge had scribbled, "They know. Get out."

My heart sank down to my knees as I dropped the note into the bowl and flushed, waiting just long enough to be sure it went down. Then, I stepped out and went to the sink. The water took a minute to warm, and I used that time to think quickly. There were no windows in here, so I couldn't improvise a signal and hope to get help. We were going to have to get back out there. I just hoped they didn't know we knew. If only I knew who "they" were . . .

"Are you guys coming up to the dining hall for lunch? I'd

love to have you as our guests." Renee's voice was casual, but all the hairs on my arms stood on end.

"Oh, we'd love that, but I thought only residents could have guests." I had no idea if that was true, but it sounded plausible. "Reverend Villay mentioned lunch when we visited the compound."

Renee opened the door for us, and as we walked back into the vestibule, she said, "That's true. But Scott moved up there this week." She smiled sweetly. "See you up there. Dinner starts"—she looked at the clock over the door—"in fifteen."

Mika and I both nodded and then watched her walk over to Scott, who gave us a wave and a smile, before putting his arm around Nadia and steering her to the door. Nadia looked back over her shoulder to us, and I sucked in a quick breath. I knew what Sawyer's face looked like when he was scared, and that little girl was terrified.

We couldn't leave her up there with those people, especially if they were onto us. I scanned the room for Marge, but I didn't see any sign of her. I hoped that meant she had made her own getaway, but, somehow, I doubted it.

I located the light switch by the door, but it was blocked by a group of men. I thought maybe I could fake that I tripped and still get to the switch, but the thought of Nadia's fear stopped me.

Mika and I made a show of picking up cookies and getting coffee, and then we tucked ourselves into a corner. "What do we do?" Mika asked. "We can't abandon Marge."

"Or Nadia," I added. "Did you see her?"

"Poor girl looked like she wanted to cry. She's so scared of her uncle."

I forced down a bite of cookie and chased it with a swig of surprisingly good coffee. "We have to go up there," I said.

Mika nodded. "Agreed, but we also have to find a way to let Santiago or your dad know what's going on."

A few of the men in the room had turned to watch us, so I said, "My phone is in the car. Maybe we'll have signal and can let them know."

"Worth a shot," Mika said as she smiled and headed toward the door. I trailed behind and watched the light switch as I walked by. I hoped this wasn't going to go horribly wrong.

12

We hurried to the car as quickly as we could without running, and as we went, I wished Dad and I had devised a language that I could use while we walked. Maybe something like base coaches or catchers in baseball use with nose tugs and arm rubs.

Once we had the doors closed, I grabbed my phone and groaned when I saw it had no bars. Mika shook her head. She didn't have any signal, either.

"Okay, so we need to go with the kidnap-victim plan then," I said with an attempt at levity. "A note in the car window so that they can see it as we drive by."

"Isn't that risky?" Mika asked. "I mean, other people might see it, too."

I sighed. "Yeah, but do you want to go up there without our backup understanding the situation?"

"No. Okay, what do I write?" She had a tube of bright-red lipstick and a napkin already in her lap.

"Where did you get those?" I said with a chuckle. "Doesn't look like your color."

She smiled. "It isn't. I was going to use it the next time I babysat Sawyer. He loves to paint my face with lipstick, and I thought this would be fun."

"And the napkin?" I said as I let myself think of my son for just a moment.

"Your glove box. I always shove extras in there when we get fast food. Don't you do that?"

"You forget, when I get fast food, Sawyer is with me. I need every napkin I can get at the moment." That boy had never yet had a milkshake that didn't end up half in the seat.

"I suppose 'we've been made' is a little obvious, huh?"

I nodded. "Probably. Maybe something like, 'Couldn't get the switch. Will try the one upstairs.' Could someone think that's a personal note about my house or something?" I knew I was grasping at straws, but I had to try to hold onto something. I was flipping terrified.

"I like it." She wrote the phrase in big, clear letters and handed it to me as she capped the lipstick. "Side window maybe?"

I was just spinning around to affix it to the back window behind my seat when someone knocked beside my ear. I looked up to see Nick Sterit looking at me.

Quickly, I slid the note onto the dashboard and pretended to wipe up a spill with another before I turned the key and let the window down. "Hi, Mr. Sterit," I said. "We were just on our way up to the dining hall. Scott and Renee invited us, too. Is that okay?"

He grinned. "More than okay. Let me give you a ride. Save you the gas and the trouble." Before waiting for my answer, which was going to be a big no-thank-you, he opened my car door and extended his arm. The act might have seemed kind, even chivalrous, if it didn't make my entire body go cold with fear.

I glanced at Mika, and she looked to her side of the car, where another man was moving to open her door. She looked back at me, and we both moved to step out. We didn't really have a choice.

Each of the men took our hands and put them on their forearms, and for a very fleeting second, I felt like I was in a Jane Austen novel. Then, I saw the brown pickup waiting for us, and all illusions of Victorian gallantry went zooming off into the sunset.

I glanced around, hoping that my dad and Lucille were close enough to see what was happening. On the spur of the moment, I decided I needed to give them a little more to go on and reached into the pocket of my skirt, where I'd dropped my keys out of habit. "Just let me lock my car?" I said to Nick as I stopped.

I pushed the button and heard the sequence of beeps signaling the doors were unlocked. Then, I dropped my keys back into my pocket and said, "All set." Then, I began to pray that Lucille had heard the sound and knew what it meant.

Nick held the passenger's side door open and let me slide in. Mika followed, and then her escort climbed in beside her. Nick got behind the wheel, and suddenly, I was in some sort of rural nightmare where four of us were squeezed into a bench seat with a gun rack on the window behind me.

Mika and I held hands like petrified schoolgirls again, and as we entered the compound road, I felt my breaths getting more and more shallow. I forced myself to think about Sawyer, to consider the beauty of the forest around us, and to breathe deeply. It wouldn't do for me to pass out before we arrived. We were already vulnerable enough without a loss of consciousness.

The distance was probably only three miles, but it felt like it took forever to get there. I was uncomfortably pressed against Santa Man, and the car was too warm. Plus, terror has a way of making everything more unpleasant. Still, when we arrived at the dining hall, I started to feel the panic rising again. What if no one had seen us leave? What if they didn't have time to get here before . . .

I forced myself to stop that line of thought and, instead, concentrated on playing my part. "It's so beautiful here," I said and meant it. If it wasn't for the woman-hating cult and the fact that a possible murderer was living on the premises, I might have indeed wanted to move here.

"One of the reasons the reverend picked this spot," the man who was once again holding Mika's arm said.

She smiled up at him and said, with innocence that would make a puppy look sinister, "What were his other reasons?"

The man smiled and said, "Privacy was the big one, and—"

Santa Man cut him off. "Let's go in, shall we?" he said as he opened the glass door and ushered us in.

Inside, it felt like a throwback to the eighties. The walls were paneled, and the floor space was filled with the exact same style of cafeteria table that I'd had in high school. For a fleeting second, I thought about looking under one of the ones with the blue stools attached to see if my initials were still carved underneath.

As we came in, Renee greeted us with hugs, and Scott even came up and put out his hand. "No hard feelings," he said with not one ounce of sincerity.

Santa Man turned me around toward the wall next to the door through which we'd come and said, "We're so glad you could be here for our memorial, ladies."

On the wall above a table featuring a massive arrangement of chrysanthemums hung a banner that read, "In Memory of Stephen Sutherland. May he rest in peace."

My stomach dropped as I turned to look at Mika. She looked like she might pass out, so I quickly slipped my arm around her waist as I said, "Oh, isn't that lovely?"

I felt a hand come to rest on my shoulder. "I'm glad you think so, Paisley, because this is all inspired by you."

Reverend Villay's voice was syrupy sweet and undercut with menace. As I turned to look at him, the gleam in his eye told me all I needed to know about what he was thinking. This man knew everything, and he didn't care if we knew, too.

When I looked back to Renee and Scott, they were both grinning, but not with delight. The anger shone in the hard rounds of their cheeks, and I understood, for the first time, why some people were so terrified of clowns. Smiles that were not genuine were scary things.

"Please, come sit," the Reverend said, and our escorts pulled us toward a table with two place settings. "We have a great meal planned for you. I think you'll really enjoy it."

I tried to resist sitting, but Santa Man's hands pushed down on my shoulders until I dropped onto the stool. Next to me, Mika was forced into her own seat. "Now, I hope you like pot roast because the women have been cooking all day."

At that moment, four women, teenage girls really, appeared at a swinging door on the other side of the room, and each of them had a dish full of food in their hands. Pot roast with potatoes and carrots and what looked like a large salad. I'd had this meal recently with Mary after church, and it had been so delicious. In this moment, though, I decided I'd never eat pot roast again, starting now.

Mika shot me a glance, and I shook my head slightly and said in a hiss, "Don't eat."

She shook her head again and swallowed hard enough for me to see her throat move.

Then, the women were at the table and filling our plates. The food did smell delicious, but I didn't trust it. I knew Jim Jones and the Narrow Gate stories. I wasn't eating or drinking anything served by a cult, especially not when I was, it seemed, the guest of honor.

The doors opened behind us, and a stream of people came in to form a circle around us. It felt like a nightmare – all their faces were so still. Some people looked scared; some very angry. Some just placid and disaffected. They were the scariest of all.

I scanned the crowd and caught Marge's eyes. She shook her head and looked pointedly at the food. I gave a slight nod. We were on the same page about the meal, then. I didn't know if that was good or bad, and I wasn't sure whether to feel relieved or terrified that Marge was still there. I decided I'd take it as a gift that she was at least still alive.

"Let us say a prayer of thanks," Reverend Villay said, and everyone joined hands. Santa Man grabbed my hand, and his fingers were so soft they felt slimy. Fortunately, Mika's grip was strong on my other fingers.

"Heavenly Father," the pastor began, "thank you for the opportunity to gather in your name." The prayer went on for some time with platitudes about thankfulness and guests, but I was only paying attention with a tiny part of my mind because the rest of it was scanning for a way out. I wasn't coming up with anything, nothing at all.

My attention snapped back to the prayer when the reverend said, "Thank you that our ordeal with Brother Stephen has ended. Thank you that we now do not need to live in fear of discovery any longer. Thank you for providing us a way. In your name, Amen."

I took a deep breath and decided I just needed to go for broke here. If we were going to die, which seemed likely, I had to hope that maybe just knowing what had happened to Stephen would ease my passing. "What happened to Stephen Sutherland?"

The people around us shot glances at one another, but when Reverend Villay spoke, the entire room went quiet. "Stephen, unfortunately, found himself in a place that was too dangerous for him, and that place killed him."

"You mean, you killed him," Mika said clearly. "You and

your cronies killed him because he was poking around and found your secrets."

"He wasn't minding his own business!" Renee spat before she gritted her teeth and glared at Mika.

Reverend Villay put up a steady hand. "No, Sister. We don't need to disparage the dead." Then he turned to Mika and me. "Stephen found himself with some information that was dangerous. Steps were taken to be sure that information never went beyond him."

"Come on, Reverend Villay. Be a man and admit what you did." I was surprised the words had come out of my mouth, but when I saw the look of shock on Villay's face, I smiled. He wasn't used to being talked to that way, particularly by a woman, I expected. "Tell the truth."

The sneer that crossed the pastor's face sent a chill down my spine, but he quickly pulled his mask of calm leadership back into place and said, "The truth is that sometimes the greater good requires great sacrifice."

"You really aren't able to speak plainly, are you?" I refused to break eye contact with him.

"What do you wish I would say, Ms. Sutton?" His voice was calm but clear.

"Did you kill Stephen Sutherland?"

"I did not." He smiled beatifically and started to turn from me.

But I wasn't an idiot. "I believe you. Did you order his murder?"

I heard a hiss from the other side of the circle but didn't dare turn to look at who made the sound.

Reverend Villay's eyes snapped back to mine, and he moved toward me. "Since you will not be sharing this information with anyone, I will tell you what you want to know. Maybe then, you can rest in true peace."

The irony that I had just thought the same thing wasn't lost on me, so I just smiled and said, "Thank you."

"I asked some of my church members to address our information problem as best they saw fit and asked them to do it permanently." A self-satisfied smile crossed his face. "When it became clear that Stephen was problematic for our private lives here, I asked them to take care of things. So yes, I ordered that Stephen Sutherland be killed."

I'm pretty sure my mouth fell open because I didn't actually think he'd admit it.

"Now, again, please enjoy your meal. And while you eat, I will give you some assurances that will, I hope, further increase the calmness you feel."

I glanced at Mika and then turned to Renee and Scott. "You played me!" I said quietly. I wanted to shout, but all the fight had gone out of me. "You set up that whole scene at the park?"

Renee shrugged. "You're a soft-hearted woman, Paisley. I couldn't have known how well you'd tie things up, though. Taking me to Mika's shop so that she became part of the story, well, that was just too perfect."

I felt tears prick my eyes. I had brought Mika into all of this, and now her death was going to be my fault.

Scott raised his eyebrows and said, "I really do play the part well."

"I doubt you had to play a part at all," Mika snapped. "Came pretty naturally, as I understand it."

Reverend Villay stepped into my line of vision. "All of that is in the past. As I said, I'd like to give you some assurances about the future, if you don't mind. Please, though, do eat. It's the least painful option you have ahead of you."

I think it was in that moment that I realized we were well and truly out of options. We were surrounded by dozens of people, many of whom probably had weapons. We were miles away from a vehicle and had no cell signal. And obviously, no one had gotten our message and come to rescue us.

I felt the saddest about that last one because I'd have hoped that Dad and Santiago would have come anyway when they saw us ride off, but maybe they interpreted our lack of signal as a stand-down. I tried to focus on the fact that they were safe so that I wouldn't feel betrayed.

"Your son, Ms. Sutton, will always be safe. As long as no one takes any further action against us, he can live with your ex-husband – sorry about that, by the way – without interference from us." Reverend Villay's voice was so patronizing that I wanted to punch his teeth in. Actually, I wanted to punch his teeth in for even thinking about harming my son. Mika put her hand on my arm, though, and that stopped me from jumping up and, probably, ending my life right then.

"Your father and stepmother will not be harmed either, again, unless they interfere. Your father thinks the world of you, as I do of my daughters"—his eyes flicked to two young girls just to his left—"so we will tell him that you had a terrible accident here and make it clear that as long as he doesn't get nosy, his grandson will remain fine. No need to take more action than necessary. Right, Nicholas?"

"Understood," Santa Man said.

"Well, you could offer the same deal to us," Mika squeaked. "Neither of us will say anything. You have our word."

I knew she meant what she said, and I also knew it would do no good.

"I'm afraid, Ms. Andrews, that we must make an example of someone for the women in our community. It simply won't do for anyone to go thinking they can interfere without punishment. His eyes moved slowly to Marge, and she took a step back.

He flicked his eyes back to us. "Now, then, I must insist you eat," Reverend Villay said. "Or else, we'll need to have the gentlemen here take you for a walk in the woods."

I almost laughed because taking us for a walk in the woods sounded so cliché, like a hillbilly mafia line, but the reverend's face was completely placid. Somehow that was more terrifying than if he looked angry or even frustrated.

I went to pick up the fork in front of me because I figured I could at least try to fake eating, maybe drop some bites in my lap to buy a bit more time. I was just about to let the first piece of potato slide to the floor when I heard a familiar voice say, "Stop right there, Paisley. Don't even think about it."

Mika's head jerked up and swiveled around until she found him. "Uncle Saul, what are you doing here?"

"Oh, I go to church here, have for quite some time." His face was stern, and I couldn't get a read on what was going on. "Put your forks down, girls."

I set my fork against my plate, prongs down at five o'clock. A small homage to my etiquette teacher who said that this placement of your fork signaled that you were done with your meal. I had no idea why my brain remembered that tiny tidbit from a decade earlier in that most terrifying moment, but there it was . . . and I hoped I didn't actually have to pick that fork up again.

Saul stepped toward Reverend Villay and put out his hand. "Pastor, thank you for inviting my niece and her friend here today. I think it's wise to have them in this space, to bring them closer so that we can tie up any loose ends."

I swallowed hard and felt tears in my eyes. When I looked up at Mika, all the color had drained from her face, and she was staring, open-mouthed, at her uncle. I quickly grabbed her hand and squeezed her fingers tight.

Reverend Villay put out his hand and shook Saul's, and in that instant, the entire room erupted. Saul spun the pastor and put him in a headlock as Dad and Lucille charged from one side of the room and Santiago and his deputies from the other. Most of the women and some of the men scattered, but Santa Man, the creepy guy who had brought Mika in, and Renee and Scott were in handcuffs before I could even get to my feet.

I turned toward Mika, and she was standing beside me and spinning around slowly. "What just happened?" she said.

"I think Saul was a plant. Maybe. I think. I don't know." I turned to Santiago, who had handed up Reverend Villay to Officer Layton and was heading my way. "You got our message."

"Smart move with the light switch note. We would have seen you come and followed, but given the note, we realized we needed to get in here, and quick." He stepped forward and pulled me tight to his chest. For just a second, I let myself feel all the panic that had been rising in me since this morning, but then, I squelched it back down in favor of getting more information. "But Saul?"

"Yeah, Uncle Saul, what is going on? Were you an undercover agent?" Mika had grabbed her uncle and was holding tight to his arm.

He slid his arm around Mika's shoulders and pulled her close. "Nothing formal or sanctioned." He looked at the sheriff and nodded. "I knew you'd been stonewalled a long time up here, and I was tired of seeing the women of this town, and the men, too, for that matter, suffer. So I just figured I'd get inside and take a look."

"So you were undercover?" Mika's voice was part awe, part reprimand. "And you didn't tell anyone?"

"Everybody knows everybody . . . couldn't risk it. Took me about three months, but I was pretty close to getting someone to talk with me." Saul looked across the room and smiled at Marge. "But then, we found Stephen's body, and you two started asking questions."

I hung my head. "We didn't know anything about the church when we talked to Olivia. Definitely didn't know they had killed Rocket." I sighed. "We didn't mean to mess up your sting operation."

Saul guffawed and smiled at me. "I don't think I'd go that far with the nomenclature, Paisley, and I know you weren't trying to interfere. If anything, I should apologize for scaring you to death when old Nick Sterit came by. The look on your face . . ." He shook his head. "I didn't know how to tell you without putting people at risk." Again, his eyes darted to Marge again, who was talking now to Officer Layton.

"I understand," I said. "I'm just glad it turned out this way and that you're not some rabid cult member who hates women."

Mika snuggled into his shoulder and said, "Me, too."

Dad and Lucille pushed their way through the group around us and grabbed me in a double-hug that nearly cracked my ribs. Dad still had his gun over his shoulder, so he also nearly broke my jaw. But I didn't care. I needed that hug. "You came?"

"Are you kidding?" Lucille said. "If the sheriff here hadn't caught us as we were headed toward the building, we would have been in here fifteen minutes ago, guns a-blazing . . . literally."

I teared up again. "I'm so glad you're here," I said, "but I'm glad you didn't come in because we did get the reverend to confess."

"And I got a recording," Mika said as she drew her phone out of her pocket. The red dot was still flashing at the bottom of the screen.

I hugged her and said, "You are so smart." Then I turned to the people around me and said, "This, friends, is why all skirts should have pockets."

13

Santiago and Officer Davenport took our statements at the station after they finished processing Reverend Villay, Santa Man, and a few others for murder. Officer Layton, Officer Dutch, and Officer Spicer were speaking, one by one, with the two dozen or so women who came in to give their statements about assault, abuse, and even rape. Apparently, the sight of their pastor in handcuffs had made them feel it was safe enough, finally, to come forward.

Mika slipped over to talk to Marge for a minute after we were done. She wanted to thank her for warning us and be sure Marge would be okay. "Please thank her for me, too," I said, and Mika nodded.

Then, I slid back into the not-so-comfy chair at the edge of the deputies' workroom and took a deep breath. It was after three now, and Sawyer would be back at my house in less than three hours. I needed to take this moment, public though it may be, to let my emotions rise up. Better here in a room full of people who knew what had happened than tonight while Sawyer and I were getting ready for bed.

The tears came, steady and quick, and at one point, I had to sit forward and put my head between my knees just to keep my sobs a bit more under control. But after a few minutes, I felt more balanced, more even, and I was able to stand up and go look for something cold to drink. I didn't drink soda often, but today was a day that called for sugar and caffeine.

I made my way into the small break room at the back of the station and dug some change out of my purse. Fortunately the soda machine stocked my favorite, Cheerwine, and I had just popped the tab on the ice-cold can when Olivia Sutherland came in. When I saw her, I pulled the can from my lips and smiled.

She rushed over and folded me into her arms. "Thank you," she said. "You found the answers."

I stepped back and set my can down on the table next to me. "I'm so sorry, Olivia." It was all I could think to say.

She nodded. "Me, too, but not for what you did. You and Mika, you got justice for Stephen. And you gave me perspective I needed to have."

I looked over her shoulder and could see Renee handcuffed to a chair at the back of the room by the wall of cells. I guessed they didn't have enough space for everyone. "I'm sorry about Renee, too."

Olivia followed my gazed. "Yeah, she bought the line a lot of us do about what we should be. She's a victim here, too, in some ways." She turned back to me. "But I'm glad she won't be at my table anymore. Nadia, though . . ."

I thought of the little girl who I'd last seen in the dining hall crying and reaching for her mom as she was put in the back of a police car. That little one was going to need a lot of help from a lot of people. "The sheriff will know what to do to help her, I'm sure."

"Oh, he did. He's working with me, and we're going to get

me approved to be a foster mother. Then, I'll do my best to adopt her, if she'll have me."

I stared at Olivia and felt tears come to my eyes again. "Even after Renee did all—"

"That little girl needs someone to love her, and I figure if Stephen had been able, he would have been that little girl's father. At least she'll have a grandmother." Olivia's jaw was set, and I had to work hard to resist the urge to hug her. Even when people proved themselves absolutely terrible, someone like Olivia came along and proved we could be amazingly good, too.

I stood and was just about to say my goodbyes when Mary Johnson came in, took one look at me, and hugged me so tight I felt like my spine touched my sternum. Then, she pushed me back at arm's length and studied my face. "You're okay?"

I let out of a long breath. "I'm okay." I sat back down. I was okay but still shaky. "Thank you for the heads-up about Renee. She was there today, and she was – well, she was something." I tried to smile, but even the thought of how fully Renee and Scott had played me left a bitter taste in my mouth.

Mary sat down across from me. "It's kind of amazing how some of us women haven't really gotten the idea that we're better when we help each other."

"Amen to that," Olivia said as she pulled out a chair. "This idea that somehow we owe men something in particular . . ." She sighed and let her head fall back. "But let's not talk about that stuff. Let's talk about you and the sheriff."

"Yes, let's," Mika said with a smile as she grabbed a chair from the next table over.

I looked at the three women sitting with me and sighed. "How did you know?" I asked Olivia.

Olivia grinned. "I knew he was interested from the minute he walked into my house."

Mary tapped the table. "I'm just hearing about this situation, but I don't need anything more than the look on your face to see you're sweet on him, too." She glanced over to where Santiago was talking with Officer Winslow. "And who can blame you? He is a fine man."

"And a fine-looking one, too," Mika said with a giggle. She abruptly sat up and said, "Sorry. I don't know what came over me. I think it's the ghost of the cafeteria tables up at that cult-place. It took me back to high school."

I laughed. "To be honest, I feel kind of like I did in high school when I had a crush on Doug Nichols. He was artsy and cool, and every time he came in the room, my heart rolled over." When I looked over at Santiago, he caught my eye and smiled. "See, it just did it right then," I said as I turned back to the table.

"You could do far worse, Paisley," Olivia said. "But I'm not sure you could do a lot better."

Mika took my hand. "But it doesn't matter what we think. You should do or not do when you want . . . or don't want." She put her hand to her forehead and said, "I'm tired. Do you mind giving me a lift home? I miss my bed."

I stood up and held out my hand. "Let's do this. I have a couch, a cat, and a nap waiting for me."

Olivia and Mary waved as we headed out the door. On the brief drive to Mika's apartment, I told her about Olivia's plan to foster Nadia and her hope to adopt her, and she was as thrilled as I was. "Do you ever wish you could be the person who did something like that?" I asked as I pulled to the curb.

"We're the people who captured a murderer, exposed a cult, and saved who knows how many women from terrible things. I'm going to count that as enough for one day," she said as she opened the car door. "Enjoy your nap, and really, Pais, date the sheriff or don't. Go slow or fast. Whatever you want to do . . . do that." She blew me a kiss and closed the door.

I drove away, smiling and grateful.

When I got to my house, Dad and Lucille were waiting in the living room. They'd cleaned up the entire house and left a casserole warming in the oven for my dinner. Candles were lit, and the remotes were right by the couch. Beauregard even had fresh water.

As soon as I was sat down, they put on their coats and headed for the door. At first, I started to protest, to say I wanted to talk about the day. But then, I realized that, really, all I wanted was a good cry, bad TV, and a prone position. So I thanked them and settled in under a quilt.

Two hours later, I woke up as the timer on the oven went off. Smart Lucille had set it so I'd be sure to eat and be ready before Sawyer got back. I scooped out a heaping dish of lasagna and then sat back down to watch one episode of *Mrs. Maisel.* The credits rolled just as I heard tires in the driveway. I quickly put my dish in the sink, turned on the outside light, and smiled for my little boy. Someday, I'd tell him about this weekend, but today, I just wanted to hug him, hear about his time with his dad, and get him to bed without incident.

Blessedly, the evening was easy. Sawyer was charming and quite content to play on his own, and when it came time for bed, he dropped off in moments, leaving me time to get a cup of tea and watch more *Mrs. Maisel.* About eight-thirty, a text came in: *Up for porch time?*

I smiled and wrote back: *Definitely. See you in thirty?*

With bells on . . . okay, not really.

By the time Santiago arrived, I had lit a couple of candles on the small table Dad and Lucille had given me for the front porch, and I'd made decaf Irish coffee. After today, I figured we both needed warmth and *warmth*.

"This is nice," Santiago said as he sat down and dropped the throw blanket I'd left on his chair onto his lap. "Special occasion?"

I shrugged and wrapped myself up tight in my own blanket. "Maybe."

He smiled and waited a minute, but when I didn't say more, he said, "I expect you'd like an update."

"I wouldn't mind one, but please only what you can tell me without any complications for you." I really, really didn't want to make his job harder, especially since my trying to help this time had definitely given him a lot more work to do. I didn't think he minded the work since it meant he helped the women he'd been wanting to help, but I still felt kind of guilty.

"Reverend Villay has been arrested and charged with murder, based on the recording on Mika's phone." He took a sip of his coffee. "Brilliant move, that one. Cut through all the usual he-said, she-said stuff."

"She's a smart woman." I sipped my coffee and waited for more.

"Nick Sterit and two other men will also be charged as accessories until we figure out what role, exactly, they played in Stephen Sutherland's death." He sat forward. "The tricky bit is Renee and Scott Morris. We're holding them on kidnapping charges, and the DA thinks that will stick."

"Can Renee be charged with kidnapping her own child?" I knew that was possible in custody cases, but I thought that involved crossing state lines or something.

"Not for kidnapping Nadia, Paisley. For kidnapping you and Mika. They were holding you against your will, and their ploy to draw you in was all part of that endeavor." He studied my face. "You didn't think I was going to let them get away with what they did to you, did you?"

I blushed. His voice was deep and rough, and I could hear the emotion in it. "Well, thank you. But I really am sorry for—"

"Stop, Paisley. You did a good thing today. Another time we will talk about you making better choices and avoiding dangerous situations, but today you did a good thing." He smiled and sat back in his chair.

I leaned across the small table and took his hand, where it was resting next to his mug. "Thank you, but I won't be doing that again. I'm sticking to risking my life by climbing into abandoned buildings, thank you very much." I ran my finger over his knuckles. "But I did want to take one more risk tonight."

He tilted his head and looked at our hands. "Yeah?"

"I think I'm ready," I said. "If you'd like to . . ." I felt heat rush up to my ears again.

"Go steady," he said with a smile.

I rolled my eyes. "They didn't even say that when we were in high school. What are you? Channeling our parents?"

"I'll have you know my grandmother would say I needed to court you first." He was grinning.

"What with the candle and all?"

"Yes, we could only be here together until the candle burned down, and then I'd need to go home." He held up my hand, which he was now fully enclosing in his own. "And there'd be none of this."

"Probably none of this then either, huh?" I stretched across the table and kissed him softly.

He let his mouth linger on mine and then said, "Definitely none of that."

When I made it back to my inbox on Monday morning while Sawyer held a truck-staging party with his bears and babies, I had five messages from people who hoped I could come and salvage some precious pieces of their family homes or landmarks in their communities that were to be torn down. It looked like I would be set for work for awhile, and I was particularly keen on getting into the old warehouse over the mountain that one writer had described because it had once been a printing press.

But the message that stood out most to me was from the people who owned the house where Rocket's body was found. They had decided to erect a small cairn in honor of Rocket using the remaining stones from the chimneys of the house, and they hoped I would come and be a part of the service once the monument was ready.

I replied immediately and told them that I would be honored. When I told Mika about their plan that afternoon when Sawyer and I stopped by, she was quite moved by the gesture and asked if I'd see if she could come.

"You know, they also hired Uncle Saul to finish taking down the building. They had planned to just rent a bulldozer and push it over, but because Rocket had been buried there, they wanted to be more respectful." She smiled and ruffled Sawyer's hair as he undid a skein of purple yarn.

"Oh, I like that, and I expect Saul was more than happy to oblige." It sounded like just the kind of thing he would love doing.

"He was thrilled, especially since he thinks he can get some more beams and stones for you to sell." She looked at me and grinned. "He's wondering if you want to set up a small 'boneyard' at his place."

"You mean like the Barnwood Builders do? Will Saul be Johnny Jett?" I asked with a grin of my own as I imagined him in a tank top and ponytail like my favorite cast member from the reality show.

"If you ask nicely, he just might." Mika winked.

"Sawyer, what do you think about having a life-size place to build towers and cabins?" I asked as he flew past, yarn in hand.

"Can I climb them?" he shouted over his shoulder.

"Of course you can, Love Bug. Of course you can."

Read the next of Paisley's adventures in *Hanged By A Thread* - https://books2read.com/hangedbyathread.

A FREE NOVELLA AND GREAT READS

Join my Cozy Up email group for weekly book recs & a FREE copy of *A Novel Crime*, the prequel to my St. Marin's Cozy Mystery Series.

Sign-up here - https://bookens.andilit.com/CozyUp

ALSO BY ACF BOOKENS

St. Marin's Cozy Mystery Series

Publishable By Death

Entitled To Kill

Bound To Execute

Plotted For Murder

Tome To Tomb

Scripted To Slay

Proof Of Death

Epilogue of An Epitaph

Hardcover Homicide

Picture Book Peril - Coming November 2022

Stitches In Crime Series

Crossed By Death

Bobbins and Bodies

Hanged By A Thread

Counted Corpse

Stitch X For Murder

Sewn At The Crime

Blood And Backstitches

Fatal Floss

Strangled Skein

Aida Time - Coming in January 2023

Poe Baxter Books Series

Fatalities And Folios

Massacre And Margins

Butchery And Bindings -- Coming in November 2022

Monograph and Murder - Coming in March 2023

Spines and Slaughter - Coming in April 2023

ABOUT THE AUTHOR

ACF Bookens lives in the Southwest Mountains of Virginia, where the mountain tops remind her that life is a rugged beauty of a beast worthy of our attention. When she's not writing, she enjoys chasing her son around the house with the full awareness she will never catch him, cross-stitching while she binge-watches police procedurals, and reading everything she can get her hands on. Find her at acfbookens.com.

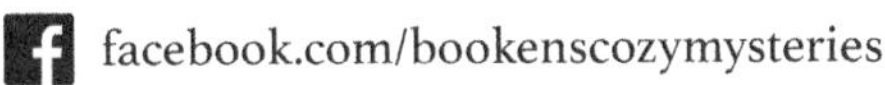